"You feel the attraction, too."

Riley wanted to refute Jackson's words, but she hated to lie. "I can't deny it. But I'm not happy about it."

"Well, I find you *painfully* attractive and it makes me *painfully* aroused. I just can't understand why a fire-breathing, tightfisted thorn in my side has me so worked up."

Riley raised her brows. "You get many dates with that kind of sweet talk?"

"I'm honest. I wanted you the instant I saw you, and even the fact that you turned out to be my worst nightmare hasn't changed that. I'll admit, at work we rub each other the wrong way. But the last thing I'm thinking about right now is work."

He drew her into his arms until they touched from chest to knee. Riley drank in the delightful sensation of his body pressing against hers.

Oh, my. He wasn't kidding about being aroused.

He lowered his head slowly toward hers, and even as she lifted her face to kiss him, she whispered, "This is so bad."

"Feels pretty damn good to me...."

Dear Reader,

Life is filled with surprises, so we need to brace ourselves—
and hope for the best. These unexpected events can range
from fabulous, like winning the lottery (hasn't happened to
me) to pleasant—hearing from an old friend with whom you'd
lost touch (has happened to me)—to not so great, like your
car breaking down on the interstate (has unfortunately
happened to me) to downright unpleasant, like discovering a
snake in the dark with your bare foot (believe me, you don't
want *that* to happen to *you*).

We've Got Tonight's hero, Jackson Lange, experiences an
unpleasant surprise when he realizes that the sexy stranger
who's just set his libido on fire is none other than his nemesis
Riley Addison. Is it possible for "unpleasant" to turn into
"fabulous"? Maybe...but Jackson and Riley will have to
discover the answer to that question themselves.

Readers often ask me where I get my ideas. The answer
is: everywhere! Music, television, newspapers all provide
inspiration. But sometimes I draw on my own life experiences,
as I did for one particular scene in *We've Got Tonight*. If you'd
like to know which scene, send me an e-mail and I'll share
the scoop. You can contact me through my Web site at
www.JacquieD.com, where you can enter my monthly contest
and find out about my latest releases.

Happy reading!

Jacquie D'Alessandro

Books by Jacquie D'Alessandro

HARLEQUIN TEMPTATION
917—IN OVER HIS HEAD
954—A SURE THING?

We've got tonight
JACQUIE D'ALESSANDRO

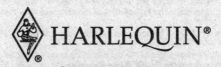

HARLEQUIN®

TORONTO • NEW YORK • LONDON
AMSTERDAM • PARIS • SYDNEY • HAMBURG
STOCKHOLM • ATHENS • TOKYO • MILAN • MADRID
PRAGUE • WARSAW • BUDAPEST • AUCKLAND

This book is dedicated with my love and gratitude to Brenda Chin,
for being a fabulous editor, a tireless cheerleader, and for
remaining calm in the face of life's little disasters. If only she
possessed a short memory, she'd be absolutely perfect. Xox

And, as always, to my wonderful husband, Joe, for never failing to be
my guiding light, and my terrific son, Christopher, aka Guiding Light, Jr.

ISBN 0-373-69199-8

WE'VE GOT TONIGHT

www.eHarlequin.com

Printed in U.S.A.

Prologue

RILEY ADDISON froze with her coffee cup halfway to her lips, then leaned forward in her office chair to re-read the company e-mail from Jackson Lange, better known as the Bane of her Existence.

Will require double the budget your department allotted, i.e. a one-hundred-percent increase, effective immediately. See attached spreadsheet for details. Contact me if any questions.

Riley's brows hiked up, and with a humorless laugh, she shook her head. The new head of Prestige Residential Construction's marketing department was clearly insane. The terse, robotic way in which Jackson Lange communicated via e-mail and on the phone convinced her he'd lived a previous life as some sort of despotic dictator who barked out orders and expected the troops to fall meekly into line.

"Well, you've picked the wrong person to bark at this time," she muttered. "Today I'm giving out asswhuppings and chocolate cookies, and sadly for you, I'm fresh out of chocolate cookies."

The only saving grace for Riley was that Prestige's marketing department was located in the company's New York offices, while her accounting department was in Atlanta—a safety buffer of over nine hundred miles that prevented her from having to deal with the intolerable Jackson Lange in person.

She blew out a long sigh and rubbed her throbbing temples to alleviate the headache that had plagued her ever since Prestige had hired Lange. Had it been only just a few short weeks ago when all had been right and rosy with her working world? Yes. Then Jackson Lange had barreled—or was slithered a more apt description?—into Prestige's New York office and all hell had broken loose.

With the longtime head of marketing retiring, Riley, along with everyone else in her department, had known changes were inevitable. But Riley had expected a Prestige employee would be promoted to the position. So much for expectations. Instead, Jackson Lange was hired from the outside. Company scuttlebutt was that Lange had a reputation in the industry as a barracuda who wasn't afraid to chew on a few people on his way to the top. Rumor also had it that he was brought in because he had connections to Elite Commercial Builders—a company the residential-based Prestige's CEO was interested in acquiring.

All the turmoil surrounding Lange's hiring led to a newfound tense work environment that Riley resented. From day one Jackson Lange had instigated changes to procedures that had been in place for years. He'd made abrupt, peremptory demands, and thoroughly disrupted the formerly cordial working balance between the accounting and marketing departments. She'd been forced to tolerate a man she so far found intolerable, and with each passing day the situation grew worse.

But she was particularly upset because as demanding as her job was, her career provided the only calm in the storm her personal life had become since her younger sister, Tara, had moved in with her after their mother's death. At work, Riley knew what she was doing. Numbers, financial statements, budgets—all that she understood. Away from the office, however, her responsibilities made her constantly feel as if she were walking a tightrope above a deep, dark canyon without benefit of a safety net. She needed a break, a change. And she needed it *now*.

Unfortunately *now* she had to deal with this e-mail from Lange, despite the fact that she'd already told him last week that no budget increase would be coming his way. "I.e. a one-hundred-percent increase," Riley muttered. "As if I don't know what *double* means. Insulting jerk."

"Uh-oh," said a familiar voice from the doorway. "You're talking to yourself. And wearing your 'Jackson Lange' killer glare. Is it safe to enter?"

Riley's gaze lifted to Gloria Morris, head of Prestige's information technology department. Dressed in a tailored, vivid turquoise dress that hugged her slim figure, with a sleek auburn bob brushing her shoulders, Gloria looked fresh and perky, and totally dispelled the typical image of the nerdy IT computer geek. Gloria was the only woman Riley knew who always looked as if she just stepped out of some exclusive salon. She loved her best friend in spite of that annoying trait.

"Safe to enter? Depends. Do you want your blood pressure to soar into the danger zone? The veins on your forehead to pop out and throb?"

"Not especially, but since you clearly could use some cheering up, I'll risk it." Gloria settled herself in the black leather chair opposite Riley. "So what's the Barracuda done now?"

"The usual—barked out peremptory demands. Only this time, he hit me before I'd finished my first cup of coffee."

Gloria shook her head. "Clearly he has no idea how grumpy you are pre-caffeine."

"Clearly not, although I wasn't grumpy until I opened Lange's e-mail. Unfortunately, I suspect my mood isn't going to improve after I look at his attached spreadsheet."

"Ooh, a spreadsheet, too. Must be your lucky day."

"Oh, yeah, lucky. That's what I'm feeling right now."

Gloria tilted her head and gave a quick, assessing look. "I don't think so. You look…tired. Droopy."

Riley sighed. "Much as I hate to admit it, you're right. I almost hung an 'out of order' sign on my bathroom mirror this morning." She shot Gloria an apologetic look. "Sorry for being a grump. In my efforts to appear outwardly calm and collected to my staff, I let all my frustrations out on you."

"Which is what friends are for. Lord knows I bend your ear enough." A teasing light lit her eyes. "I'm just not as grumpy about it as you are."

Riley laughed. "I know. I'm Grumpy, you're Happy. Throw in a poison apple and an enchanted mirror and we'd have a fairy tale."

"I'd rather throw in a handsome prince instead."

"Wouldn't we all. Although, at this point, I'd be happy just to meet someone who *interested* me."

"Interested your mind—or your body?"

"Well, both would be nice. But if I had to choose? Definitely my body."

"Amen, sister. But a somewhat surprising answer from you, Ms. Cautious and Conservative."

Riley winced inwardly at the title, as she knew it didn't aptly describe her—at least not the *real* her, but instead only the Riley she'd forced herself to become after Tara moved in. Her willful, impressionable younger sister had badly needed a good example to follow, so Riley had made certain her own behavior couldn't be called into question. But now that Tara had finally graduated from college and had announced she was moving out in two weeks, the fun-loving, sometimes wicked, sometimes daring Riley she'd ruthlessly suppressed was straining at the reins to break free.

"Actually, you're being generous," Riley said, "since Ms. Dull and Boring is closer to the truth. I've been giving this a lot of thought lately, and I realized that I've devoted so much of my personal time and effort to dealing with Tara, I've…lost part of myself in the process."

Part of Riley felt like a traitor saying the words out loud, but there was no denying the truth. When was the last time she'd done something just for her? She couldn't recall. How many times over the past five years had she cancelled plans in order to rescue her high-maintenance sister from whatever mess she'd gotten herself into? It seemed as if every event in Tara's life fell into the realm of either Crisis or Havoc-Wreaking. Missing classes because she was hungover. Cutting classes for the hell of it. Being pulled over by campus police. Forced to pull all-nighters because she'd procrastinated on assignments. Her college friends showing up at the apartment or calling at all hours of the night. Crying breakups, make-out sessions, staying out all night, parties that got out of control. All events that Riley found frustrating and exhausting, especially since her sister was stubborn about learning from her mistakes.

She blew out a long breath. "In my attempt to provide a good example for Tara, I feel like my sparkle and sense of fun have been smothered under an avalanche of responsibility."

Gloria reached out and squeezed her hand. "You're a wonderful sister, Riley, and thanks to your patience, love and understanding, Tara's finally gotten her act together. So now it's time to enjoy yourself again. You're *allowed* to enjoy yourself, Riley."

"Oh, I agree. And believe me, I'm primed to throw off my Ms. Dull and Boring shroud and turn into a freewheeling bachelorette. I'm going to let the Riley who's been buried the past five years spread her wings and fly. I'm tired of being twenty-eight and acting like I'm one hundred and eight." Feeling like a boulder was slowly lifting off her shoulders, she waggled her brows at Gloria. "And what better time to start than today? Fridays are always great days to make fresh starts—just in time for the weekend."

"And this weekend is perfect," Gloria agreed. "We're going to the baseball game tonight, and we'll have a great time working at the Children's Charity Carnival tomorrow—both perfect opportunities for scoping out available male talent. And then there's the dinner at Marcus Thornton's lake house Sunday afternoon—no potential there since it's all co-workers, but still, we'll have fun."

Riley sipped her coffee and nodded. The Braves game tonight. As a diehard baseball fan, that was definitely something fun to look forward to, as was Sunday at the CEO's gorgeous lake house. And tomorrow was Prestige's annual carnival to support local children's charities—a much-anticipated event. Now in its twenty-third year, the carnival had grown from a small affair started by Prestige's founder, Marcus Thornton, into a huge extravaganza, taking up a good part of Piedmont Park's expansive grounds. Complete with rides, games, food, silent and live auctions, music and dancing, the all-day event drew huge crowds, and a large percentage of Prestige's employees volunteered to run the various booths. Last year's carnival had netted over four hundred thousand dollars in contributions.

"I'm really looking forward to the carnival," Riley said with a smile. "All sorts of opportunities to meet eligible men there, especially since I'm working the fortune-teller's tent this year. Never know who might drop in for a palm reading."

"Lucky you. I'm working the cotton candy booth, so I'll only get pre-schoolers. Expect me to mosey on over to your tent for a reading. I want to know if I should expect a Prince Charming—or the poison apple."

Riley pressed her fingertips to her temples and closed her eyes. "I see only good things coming your way. Non-cellulite-forming cheesecakes. Calorie-free ice creams and brownies. Fabulous new shoes."

"Hmm. All good. But how about sex?" Gloria asked, an unmistakably hopeful note in her voice. "Do you see any sex on the horizon?"

Riley opened her eyes and adopted a deep, serious voice. "Madame Sees-All envisions much for you. But you will have to wait and visit my tent tomorrow to find out." She winked. "And pay your five bucks like everyone else."

"Spoken like a true accountant. And what does Madame Sees-All predict for herself?"

Again Riley touched her temples. "Hmm. I see a…rebirth. I see packing away cautious and conservative. Embracing wild and daring. I see…sex. Yes, lots of steamy, sweaty sex with a beautiful man who will not use the words 'dull and boring.' Or 'droopy.'"

"Hey—that's the fortune *I* wanted! I demand a refund."

"You haven't paid yet."

"Oh. Well, when I do, I want a fortune like yours. I haven't had a date in almost a month."

Riley didn't point out her own even more depressing statistic—she hadn't had a date in over three months. Instead, she lifted her chin with an air of determination. "I've waited a long time to take back my life, and I'm ready and eager to reembrace my fun and adventurous spirit. In fact, I feel like a stick of dynamite waiting to explode. All I need is to find the right man to light the fuse." She picked up her coffee cup and raised it in salute. "Here's to a new start. For both of us—the bachelorettes. Filled with adventure. Daring. Fun. No dull and boring."

"Or droopy," Gloria agreed, raising her own mug.

Feeling freer than she had in a long time, Riley clicked her mug's rim to Gloria's and smiled.

Let the games begin.

1

JACKSON walked slowly through Atlanta's Piedmont Park, taking in the sights and sounds of Prestige's Children's Charity Carnival while humming his pleasure over what were undeniably the best funnel cakes he'd ever eaten. Colorful balloons, the squeals of excited kids pulling parents toward game booths, the whirl of the carousel, the roller coaster and the Ferris wheel, the tantalizing scents wafting through the air from the food stalls—it was a huge operation, and based on the size of the crowd, a very successful one. A frisson of pride eased through him that he worked for a company so committed to the community and to helping children, and he was glad he'd taken up Marcus Thornton on his invitation to spend a few days in Atlanta. Not that Jackson would have refused the CEO—but this particular weekend seemed the perfect time.

His only regret was that the event was scheduled to end in only two hours and, thanks to severe thunderstorms in New York which had delayed his flight for hours, he'd only just arrived at the park. His first order of business had been to eat, and he hadn't wasted any time appeasing his hunger with a savory sausage-and-pepper hero washed down with an ice-cold beer. He popped another warm, sugary bit of funnel cake in his mouth and groaned in satisfaction.

After polishing off the last bite of his treat, he wiped the sugar from his fingers, then continued walking around the grounds. Lots of families with kids in tow. Lots of couples holding hands, laughing, playing the arcade games. His gaze settled on one snuggling couple who vaguely reminded him of Shelley and Dave. His sister and her husband of five years were incredibly happy, a fact he'd witnessed once again at Shelley's birthday party last night. Seeing them together—hugging, kissing, teasing, laughing—had filled him with an odd, wistful feeling he couldn't name. He was happy for them, but at the same time he envied them that happiness and wanted it for himself.

And clearly Shelley wanted it for him, as well, because she'd invited not one, not two, but three single co-workers, not to mention her neighbor's unmarried daughter to the party to meet him. All four women had been pleasant and attractive. Not one of them had interested him enough to want to see them again.

Damn. He seriously needed to get himself out of this funk. It wasn't as if he still mourned last year's breakup with Kimberly, but still, none of the women he'd met since really wowed him. Even the ones he'd taken to bed had only satisfied him physically. And why the hell wasn't that enough? It used to be—but not anymore. None of those women had inspired that spark that Shelley and Dave shared. That his parents shared. And that's what he wanted.

But he was tired of being the guy everyone was trying to fix up. He was a young, financially secure bachelor, and it was about time he started having some fun again. Sure, his career was his top priority, but that didn't mean it had to be his *only* priority. He sure as hell wouldn't find a spark-inducing woman by living like a monk.

After Kimberly had broken off their engagement, he'd forced himself, as a matter of pride, back into the dating pool, but he wasn't enjoying the swim. Too many time-consuming hassles and games and disappointments. His commitment to his career didn't leave much time for socializing, but damn it, he was growing tired of being, well…lonely. Yet meeting someone who really grabbed his interest was proving a daunting challenge.

Brian kept bugging him to go club-hopping, but his twenty-three-year-old brother's "go for as many hot babes as you can" dating philosophy didn't intersect on any plane with Jackson's. And besides, he was really weary of the club scene. Still, if he didn't start dating in earnest soon, Mom and Shelley would make good on their threat to start cold-calling women from the Manhattan phone directory to set him up.

Of course, part of the reason behind everyone's matchmaking efforts was Mark's upcoming wedding. Sheesh. Why did one wedding always have to beget another one? The instant his brother had announced he was getting married, Mom and Shelley had cast their matchmaking eyeballs in Jackson's direction. Brian had already offered Jackson a month's salary to remain single so "the mother and the sister stay off my back."

Well, he'd worry about that after he returned to New York. He planned to stay in Atlanta through Monday to meet some of the Atlanta staff members—one of whom would be Riley Addison.

Jackson bit back the growl of irritation that rumbled in his throat at the mere thought of the woman, as an image of the Wicked Witch of the West rose in his mind. She hadn't bothered to answer his e-mail regarding the budget increase, which irked him, but wasn't really a surprise. He was well aware that marketing and accounting departments notoriously feuded in corporations across America—marketing wanted to spend and accounting wanted to save. Still, he'd never come across anyone as tightfisted, not to mention as annoying, brusque or autocratic as Riley Addison.

As the "new" guy hired from the outside, he'd expected to face some initial resentment and hostility and he'd caught on from Ms. Addison's very first terse e-mail that their relationship wouldn't be filled with warm fuzzies. Fine. In his relentless quest to rise to the top of the corporate heap, he was used to that. But in that first e-mail she'd demanded a written explanation for a $743.82 dinner expense he'd submitted, suggesting he consult the company handbook regarding "exorbitant" expenditures. He certainly didn't need a degree in hieroglyphics to read her hidden code that she obviously believed his dinner charge was suspect and had every intention of busting his balls about it.

Damn it, that had pissed him off. Not so much that she was busting his balls—he'd expected that. But he resented that his integrity was being called into question. Like he'd tried to charge through some bogus dinner. He'd been very happy to fire off an equally terse explanation, pointing out that their *boss* had suggested he wine and dine those clients at that particular pricey restaurant.

Oh, yeah, he looked forward to meeting Riley Addison on Monday and putting her in her place face-to-face. Maybe he'd even personally hand her his expense report for his weekend trip to Atlanta. Watch her eyeballs bug out when she got a load of the "had-to-purchase-the-ticket-with-less-than-seven-days-notice-due-to-last-minute-invite-from-boss" airfare. Heh, heh, heh.

Cheered by the thought, he continued touring the grounds and tried his hand at a few games. The next hour flew by as Jackson threw baseballs at milk bottles, tossed basketballs through hoops, and won a stuffed pink hippo at the ringtoss booth. Not the most masculine of prizes, but what the heck. He tucked the stuffed animal under his arm and continued along. At the end of the last row of game booths stood a blue-and-white striped, enclosed tent. A hand-painted sign near the flap read: *Palm Reading. Discover the secrets of your future within…if you dare. Ten minutes/$5 charge.*

Jackson grinned, headed toward the tent and stood at the end of the short line. He'd attended enough carnivals and fairs to know how these things worked. Women were told they'd meet the love of their lives. Men were told they'd meet the woman of their dreams. Everyone was told they'd come into some money. It was all in fun, and in this case, for a good cause.

When it was his turn, he handed the attendant a five-dollar bill, then pushed aside the tent flap and stepped inside. His senses were instantly inundated with a heady, spicy scent that reminded him of mulled cider. A soft golden glow emanated from dozens of candles of various sizes set in crystal hurricane lamps, bathing the interior with a gilding of warmth.

A circular table covered with a glittery, jewel-toned cloth, along with two empty chairs, sat in the center of the tent.

Just beyond the table, swathed in a shimmering glow of light, stood a woman wearing a gypsy costume. Their eyes met, and Jackson stilled at the gut-level wallop of lust that sucker punched him.

For several long seconds, they simply stared at each other, and Jackson was eternally grateful for whatever internal mechanism kept his lungs operating on their own because he seemed to forget how to breathe. She was…incredible. Shoulder-length, dark glossy curls that looked sensually mussed, as if by a lover's hands. Wide-spaced eyes—he couldn't tell their color—that reflected the same surprise and interest he knew were reflected in his own.

His gaze drifted lower, lingering on her full, rosy mouth that reminded him of ripe berries, before taking in the creamy skin exposed by her off-the-shoulder blouse. A long, full, colorful skirt that brushed the floor completed her ensemble. She looked lush and curvy, feminine and sexy as hell, and everything male in him took immediate notice.

And then she moved.

She walked slowly forward, her skirt swishing, offering him a teasing hint of what he imagined were incredible legs. Each step was accompanied by the faint tinkling of bells that were attached to the gold chained belt draped around her hips—hips that swayed with a sinful walk.

He stood rooted to the spot, his heart slapping against his rib cage, as if he'd just played a grueling five-set tennis match. Had he just been thinking that he hadn't met any spark-inducing women? Anyone who wowed him? That meeting someone who really grabbed his interest was proving a daunting challenge? Well, so much for that. He was definitely sparked, wowed and grabbed. One look at this woman, and everything inside him proclaimed *game, set, match.*

She moved nearer and his brain shifted into fantasy mode. He imagined her coming closer...close enough to touch. To explore all those curves that looked so...explorable. Close enough for her to wrap her arms around his neck and kiss him with that gorgeous, pouty mouth. Instead she sank gracefully into one of the chairs and indicated the seat across from her with a wave of her hand—an invitation he definitely planned to take her up on as soon as he remembered how to move.

"I can't read your palm if you stand way over there," she said in a smoky voice laced with a teasing hint that instantly brought to mind tangled sheets and hot sex.

Unable to tear his gaze from hers, he forced his feet into motion and stepped forward, feeling as if he were wading through waist-deep water. He sat, setting his pink hippo on the floor, then looked across at her. And for the second time in less than a minute he felt as if the air had been knocked out of him.

She was even more incredible up close. Long lashes surrounded her eyes, which he could now tell were a golden brown that reminded him of caramel—another of his favorites. Those eyes flickered with an unmistakable heated awareness that sped up his heart rate into the danger zone. Glints of gold flashed from her large, slender hoop earrings, which he found inexplicably sexy. When the hell had he ever found a woman's *earrings* sexy? He'd walked into this tent and lost his marbles. Right before he'd been incinerated by an inferno of lust.

Her silky mess-with-me curls begged his fingers to reach out and touch, and her mouth…whew. Those glossy, full lips begged him to lean forward and taste. He drew in a much-needed breath and smelled the delicious scent of vanilla. He wasn't sure if it was her or the votive candles flickering on the table, but whichever, it had him all but salivating with the desire to nibble on her.

His common sense coughed to life and commanded that he say something before she decided he was some sort of ogling pervert. And he would have spoken, surely he would have, except just as he prepared to open his mouth to do so, she smiled. A slow, warm, flirty, sexy smile that awakened twin dimples on her cheeks and filled her eyes with a sparkly, mischievous gleam that seemed to whisper, *I know something you don't know, and I can't wait to tell you.*

Holy hell. He felt like someone had lit a match to his pants. Desire hit him like an openhanded slap, ripping heat through his veins. He couldn't recall ever experiencing such a swift, visceral punch of lust before. And based on the gleam of interest in her eyes, she was attracted to him, as well.

"There are only three things necessary for our palm reading," she said in her throaty voice, her eyes glowing with teasing warmth. "You, me—" she leaned closer to him "—and, well, your palm." She flicked a meaningful glance at the empty tabletop.

Jackson roused himself from his stupor and, with a grin, he rested his hands on the table. "Sorry. Too busy admiring the view."

Her gaze eased over him in a speculative way that had him shifting in his chair. Cripes, if this woman made him hard with a mere look, what the hell would happen when she touched him?

"Yes, the view in here just improved dramatically," she murmured when their eyes again met. "Are you right-handed or left-handed?"

She'd just knocked him on his ass and she expected him to answer these trick questions? He cleared his throat. "Right-handed. What's your name?"

She shot him a saucy wink. "You may call me Madame Sees-All."

Oh, man, he was a goner. A wink. When was the last time a woman had winked at him? He couldn't recall. Since when had a mere wink become so damn sexy?

"What's *your* name?" she asked.

"Seems a legitimate fortune-teller would know."

Her lips twitched, drawing his gaze to their glossy, ripe fullness. "Of course, Mr....hmm. Now what name suits you?"

"Mr. Thinks You're Gorgeous?" he suggested.

A wash of alluring color stained her cheeks, and his fingers itched to reach out and touch that beguiling blush.

"Rather a long name," she murmured with a smile, "but compliment duly noted and appreciated. And extended back."

Reaching out, she took his hand and lightly skimmed her fingertips over his palm. And he found out exactly what would happen when she touched him.

A heated tingle sizzled through him, and he swelled against his trousers. When had his hand turned into such a mass of sensitive nerves? And when the hell had he ever been so turned on by such a simple touch? Never. There must be something in the water in Atlanta to elicit this reaction in him. She'd barely touched him yet he felt as if he'd been hooked up to a nuclear reactor and she'd flipped the switch.

She studied his hand, slowly caressing each of his fingers, filling his head with erotic images of her soft, clever hands stroking the rest of his body. "That feels incredible," he said, leaning closer. "I think you've cast a spell on me, Madame Sees-All."

She looked up from studying his hand and gazed at him with a heat that created a firestorm of want through him. The hint of a smile teased the corner of her lips. "Glad to know I haven't lost my touch."

"You haven't," he assured her. "Your touch is one-hundred-percent pure magic."

After a lingering look, she once again lowered her gaze. While her fingers continued stroking, she said, "You have nice hands. Strong. Steady. They reveal that you have a sensible, well-organized disposition. That you're realistic, intelligent, successful, honorable and loyal."

"Glad to know they don't peg me as a bank robber."

Her dimples flashed. "The palm is like a landscape of hills and valleys," she continued in that sexy, husky voice, "with the highest parts called mounts." She gently kneaded the fleshy area below his thumb. "This is called the Mount of Venus. Yours is nicely full, meaning you have a love of good food, good wine…and funnel cakes."

Jackson raised his brows. "How do you know that?"

She reached out and brushed her index finger over his black Polo shirt, right above the spot where his heart thumped like a jackhammer. Then she nearly stopped his heart by bringing her hand to her mouth and slowly sucking her fingertip into her mouth. "Hmm. Powdered sugar," she said with a slow grin that brought another hard, swift kick of lust. "I know the symptoms. I'm a funnel cake aficionado myself."

"Ah. A kindred spirit. The funnel cakes were excellent. If I'd known you liked them, I would have saved you a piece."

"A very generous gesture. They're not easy to share."

"I guess that depends on who you're sharing with."

She smoothed her thumb over the center of his palm and he barely suppressed a groan of pleasure. "Yes, I can see right here you have a sweet tooth. But I can't tell what your particular weakness is. Chocolate?"

"I consider myself more of a doughnut man, although I've never met a brownie I didn't like."

She closed her eyes and blew out a rapturous sigh that did nothing to relieve the strangulation occurring in his pants. God. If she reacted with such passion about *brownies*, he could only imagine what she must be like in the bedroom.

"Doughnuts and brownies," she murmured in a sexy rasp that instantly banished all thoughts of food from his mind. "My two favorites. Especially when they're warm from the oven. Any other weaknesses?"

"Yeah. Big brown eyes, long, curly hair and dimples. You?"

"I've always had a thing for blue eyes, dark hair…and doughnut lovers."

"I think that makes me the most fortunate guy on the planet."

Her gaze drifted down to his mouth and he could almost feel that look, like a heated caress. After settling her warm gaze back on his, she said, "So…you would have shared your funnel cake with me?"

"Absolutely. But only because you have those dimples," he said very seriously.

"I see. So…no dimples, no doughnuts?"

His gaze roamed her lovely, flushed face. "Actually, in your case, even without the dimples I would have shared."

"Oh? Why is that?"

"The curly hair. The big brown eyes. The beautiful smile."

She laughed, robbing him of whatever remnants of his heart she hadn't already stolen. "For someone who claims he doesn't like to share his doughnuts, you're very easily persuaded out of them."

"Actually, I'm not, as anyone in my family would tell you. I've stooped to horrible levels of treachery to secure the last Boston Cream."

"Ah. So you're a treacherous sort of man?"

"No. Just determined. When I want something."

He found himself hoping she'd ask what he wanted because he could sum it up for her in one short word: you. But she didn't ask. Instead she remained silent, her gaze steady on his while she slowly caressed the length of his middle finger. The seductive caress, combined with those beautiful eyes studying his, mesmerized him.

"Well, no one could blame you for a bit of treachery with Boston Cream on the line," she said. "I've used devious methods myself when a homemade triple-fudge, chocolate-chunk brownie was up for grabs."

"Triple-fudge, chocolate-chunk? Do they taste as good as they sound?"

"It's like a brownie orgasm."

He felt as if she'd fired up a blowtorch and roasted him. "Sounds...delicious."

"Like nothing you've ever tasted before."

"I like to taste new things." An image of him running his tongue over her smooth flesh flashed through his mind. "Any chance you'd share the recipe?"

"Well, I suppose I could give you the recipe." She smiled. "But then I'd have to kill you."

"You realize you're relegating me to a sorry future filled with store-bought brownies."

"Do you know how to bake?"

"Not unless you count toasting a bagel until it's black as baking. But my sister does. Probably if I dropped to my knees and offered to wash her car for a year or two, she'd make the brownies for me."

"No wife or girlfriend who likes to bake?"

She wanted to know if he was unattached. Very encouraging. "No wife ever, no girlfriend currently. You?"

"No wife, no girlfriend," she said with a teasing smile. "No husband or boyfriend, either."

A breath he hadn't even realized he held eased from Jackson. If this woman was unattached, he could only conclude that the male population of Atlanta needed some serious glasses. But their loss was most definitely his gain.

Before he could reply, she returned her attention to his hand. "Now this," she said, tracing her fingertip across the crease in the upper part of his palm, "this is the Line of the Heart. The position and length of this line, combined with your full Mount of Venus, indicates that you have a passionate, sensual nature." She looked up and their eyes met. "That you're a generous, attentive, affectionate lover."

Another bolt of heat sizzled through him. He may have been this turned on before, but he'd be damned if he could remember when. "A very provocative statement," he murmured. Turning the tables, he clasped her hand and trailed his fingers over her palm in the same way she'd caressed him. "It seems that your Mount of Venus is full as well," he murmured, gently kneading the plush skin, "and your Line of the Heart is almost identical to mine." He fastened his gaze on hers. "Raises the interesting question of what might happen if two such passionate, sensual natures got together."

Her eyes darkened. "An interesting question, indeed," she agreed softly. Then, with a devilish grin, she gently extricated her hand from his. "But this is *your* fortune."

He leaned back and slowly splayed his fingers on the tablecloth. "Then by all means, tell me more, Madame Sees-All. I'm all yours."

"Hmm. Another provocative statement."

"I'm so glad you think so."

Shifting her gaze from his, she again peered at his palm. "Ohh. Very interesting."

"Am I about to win the lottery?"

"I'm not sure about the lottery, but it looks like you're soon to be very lucky."

"How lucky?"

"I see you with a woman. You're very attracted to her."

He smiled. "You're very good at this."

"She's very attracted to you, as well."

"This gets better and better."

"She's wearing a red dress. You're sitting close together in an intimate little nook, sharing a bottle of wine."

"Red or white?"

"She prefers white. She's telling you that she wants to make all your sensual dreams come true. And you say you want to return the favor."

He leaned forward until no more than six inches separated their mouths. "A conversation ripe with possibilities, and most definitely a statement I'd love to hear from her. And say in return. Could this intimate little nook be the bar at the Marriott where I'm staying?"

"As a matter of fact, I think it is."

"And would this goddess in the red dress be saying these things to me around midnight tonight?"

The sensual gleam in her eyes raised his temperature a good ten degrees. "Definitely a possibility."

The tent flap opened and the young man in charge of collecting the money said, "Time's up."

She leaned back and slowly slipped her hands from his. "Your time's up."

Damn. He could have stayed right where he was, looking at her, touching her, talking to her for hours. "How about I slip the attendant another five? Or a ten? Or a twenty?"

She smiled and waggled a finger at him. "Fair is fair, and there are other customers waiting. Besides, it's not necessary. I've a hunch your fortune will come true."

"Good. Otherwise I'd have to come back and demand a refund." Reaching out, Jackson snagged her hand, then brought it to his mouth, pressing a kiss to the warm, velvety skin on the inside of her wrist. She smelled deliciously like cinnamon and vanilla.

And he really liked the way her eyes darkened at the gesture.

"I've attended a lot of carnivals and sat in quite a few gypsy tents, Madame Sees-All, but this was by far the most intriguing fortune I've ever received. I'll be waiting in the Marriott bar at midnight for my woman wearing a red dress. And she can be sure I'll make all her sensual dreams come true."

She inclined her head in silent reply, a secret smile playing around the corners of her lips. After a final lingering look, he exited the tent and immediately drew in a much-needed breath. Instead of vanilla and cinnamon, the air was redolent with popcorn, pizza and a savory mixture of carnival foods. He briefly considered getting back in line to have his fortune read again, but at least a dozen people stood waiting to enter the tent, and the carnival was scheduled to end soon.

His time would be far better spent nipping back to the food booths to buy some funnel cakes. Then he'd camp outside the gorgeous gypsy's tent until the carnival ended. She'd said she liked funnel cakes, and he had no qualms about using them to entice her into being the alluring woman in the red dress with whom he was supposed to have a midnight encounter.

"I'VE BEEN DYING TO TALK to you," Riley said to Gloria, pulling her friend toward the parking lot. She'd slipped out the back entrance of her tent, then practically dragged Gloria from the cotton candy booth. They joined the crowds exiting the park and heading toward their vehicles.

Gloria didn't even attempt to stifle her yawn. "How you have the energy to talk amazes me. I'm fried." She nodded toward the bundle in Riley's arms. "Where'd you get the pink hippo?"

"One of the fortune-telling customers left it in the tent." Riley drew a deep breath. "You're not going to believe what I did."

"I'll believe it. I'm so exhausted and my feet hurt so bad, I'll believe anything."

"I not only threw off my Miss Dull and Boring shroud, I tossed it in the fire and incinerated it but good."

"Meaning?"

"Meaning I met my light-the-fuse guy. He's the most gorgeous man. I told him that I wanted to make all his sensual dreams come true, and then I wanted him to return the favor."

Gloria stopped and stared. "I don't believe you."

"I swear." Riley barely refrained from hugging herself and twirling in a circle. "It was so…liberating. I haven't felt this free, this crazy, this daring, this *young* for eons." She tugged Gloria's arm and as they continued to the car told her about her encounter with the handsome stranger.

She concluded with, "I can't explain it, Gloria," she said. "I took one look at the guy, walking in with this ridiculous hippo tucked under his arm and it was as if fireworks went off. He was gorgeous and adorable all at once. And the way he looked at me…like I was more delicious than chocolate…" Heat trembled through her at the memory. "Maybe I was so struck by him because just before he walked in, I'd been fantasizing about what sort of man I'd like to meet. Then I turned around and there he was—like he'd just stepped out of my dreams, and *whammo*. Direct hit to the libido."

"He sounds positively yummy." Gloria waggled

her brows. "Too bad he didn't stop for cotton candy instead of funnel cakes and fortune-telling. So, are you going to meet him?"

Riley drew a deep breath and frowned. "I want to, but I'm so out of practice. It's one thing to flirt with the man at a carnival. It's quite another to meet him at his hotel. I don't know anything about him."

"Sure you do. You know he has a gorgeous smile, no wife or girlfriend, isn't embarrassed to lug around a pink hippo—which, by the way, proves he has some skill at games to have won—and he likes doughnuts."

"And brownies," Riley added.

"Right. So what more do you need to know?"

"His name would be nice," Riley said in a dry tone. "If he has a prison record. But clearly I won't find that out if I don't meet him. And I can't deny I'd like to see him again. If for no other reason than to see if that initial spark was real or imagined."

"Exactly. Besides, you really should return his hippo. I bet he left it behind on purpose, hoping you'd bring it to the hotel."

"He's staying at the Marriott," Riley mused. "That means he's from out of town. Probably here attending a conference, which is a perfect setup. I could meet him in the hotel bar—a very public place—and talk to him for a while. Get to know him a bit. If I realize I don't like him, I just leave. But if I decide that that spark wasn't just my imagination and he's as yummy as I think and I'm satisfied he's a decent person, I can have my wicked way with him."

"Next thing you know, he's on a plane back to wherever he came from, never to be heard from again," Gloria agreed. "You'll have enjoyed a great, no-strings night of unbridled passion with a guy who lights your fire just sitting there."

And she'd allow her former fun-loving self to rise to the surface. Where it belonged.

An image of the handsome stranger's face—his sexy, smile, that lovely mouth, those strong, masculine hands—flashed in Riley's mind, and heat tingled through her. She glanced at her watch. Ten-fifteen. Plenty of time to go home and change her clothes, then head to the Marriott.

"Well?" Gloria asked. "What do you think?"

Riley smiled. "I think I'm very glad I own a red dress."

2

JACKSON SAT at a corner table in the dimly lit bar, nursing a beer, and looked at his watch for probably the hundredth time in the last half hour. Ten minutes past midnight. And no sign of a woman in a red dress.

He raked his hands through his hair in frustration and again cursed that he hadn't simply stayed at the fortune-telling tent and waited for her to emerge. Instead, by the time he'd returned after purchasing the funnel cakes, the tent had been empty. He'd looked for her, but no luck. So he'd done the only thing he could do—he'd returned to the Marriott, secured a table at the crowded bar that afforded him a good view of the room and then prayed she'd show up at midnight. Prayed he hadn't read her signals wrong—that the fantasy-inducing gypsy would be the woman in the red dress.

He stole another look at his watch. Thirteen minutes past midnight. Why the hell hadn't he gotten her name? Asked for her phone number? He'd walked into that tent, taken one look at her, and it was as if some valve had opened up in his neck and all his brain cells had drained from his head—most of them settling in his groin. Never had he been so instantaneously, fiercely attracted to a woman. Never had he experienced such an intense reaction—

one that made him feel like a cartoon character whose heart went *boing* and popped out of his chest. Yet what had he done? He'd let her get away.

Maybe someone at Prestige knew who she was. He instantly brightened. Hadn't Marcus Thornton mentioned that employees from the Atlanta office volunteered to work at the carnival? If so, maybe he could track down his sexy gypsy that way. Because the thought of never seeing the woman who had revved him from a lust level of zero to sixty in .04 seconds was unacceptable.

Another peek at his watch. Fourteen minutes past. Acute disappointment flooded him. Damn. It didn't look like she was going to—

The thought ended as he looked up and saw a vision in fire-engine red standing in the archway leading from the lobby. It was his gypsy, wearing a five-alarm dress that hugged her curves in a way that made him glad he was a man. Her gaze panned over the patrons, and Jackson noted that a number of the males' gazes followed her, as well.

Just then, she caught sight of him. For several seconds they simply looked at each other, and if Jackson had been able to, he would have laughed at the repeat of the same punch-in-the-gut, heart-skewering sensation he'd experienced when he'd walked into her tent. One single word reverberated through his mind: *wow*.

He stood, watching her make her way toward him through the crowd, his appreciative gaze taking in her graceful walk and the way her flared skirt flirted just above her knees, showcasing drop-dead legs that ended in strappy, sexy heels. She'd gathered her dark curls into some sort of loose, sexy knot, leaving stray tendrils trailing down her neck—just the sort of style that made him want to loosen whatever thingamabobs she'd used to secure the strands and slip all those lovely curls free from their moorings. When she arrived at the table, he reached for her hand. Raising it to his lips, he pressed a kiss against her fingertips.

"You must be the woman in the red dress with whom I'm destined to share a bottle of wine. A fortune-teller told me about you."

Riley absorbed the press of his lips, the warmth of his breath against her fingers, the unmistakable heat and admiration in his eyes, the tingling shiver racing up her arm. Her heart lurched in an exact imitation of the way it had when he'd walked into the carnival tent. Now dressed in dark trousers and a stark white dress shirt, the top button casually undone, he was even more beautiful than she remembered. Broad shoulders, trim waist, long legs. About six-one, she judged. Just right. His thick ebony hair beckoned her fingers to ruffle through it, then stroke down over his strong jaw to test the hint of an indent gracing his chin. She actually had to clench her hands from doing so.

She drew a slow, deep breath to steady her voice before she spoke. "What did this fortune-teller say about me?"

"That I was very attracted to you. She couldn't have been more accurate. And that you were attracted to me."

"Smart fortune-teller."

A slow, devastating smile spread across his face, pulsing flutters through her. Good Lord. What he could do with a smile. She couldn't wait to see what he could do with a kiss. Reaching out, she handed him the shopping bag she carried. "You left this in the tent."

He took the bag, then laughed when he saw the stuffed pink hippo inside. "Thanks. Although I'm not surprised I forgot it. The fortune-teller was very distracting."

He indicated the cozy U-shaped booth. "Would you like to sit down?"

Riley nodded, then slid into the curved leather seat, grateful because her legs felt less than rock solid. He moved in next to her and his thigh brushed hers, sending a jolt of excitement through her. While he settled the shopping bag under the table, she glanced at the bottle of white wine chilling in an ice bucket next to the table and smiled. "Did the gypsy predict I liked white wine?"

"As a matter of fact, she did. May I pour you a glass?"

"Thank you."

While he poured two glasses, Riley jotted notations in her mental list of pros and cons. On the pro side, he was gentlemanly and polite. And he'd chosen an excellent chardonnay. And he'd looked at her as if she were the most desirable woman to ever draw breath. And he had her female hormones performing back flips and pirouettes. On the con side— nothing so far. Excellent.

"To predictions coming true," he said, handing her a glass.

"To predictions coming true," Riley agreed, touching her rim to his with a quiet *ching* of crystal. She sipped, enjoying the smooth, oaky flavor sliding down her throat, cooling a bit of the heat consuming her.

She set down her glass then looked at him, and found herself trapped by his gaze. The way he was looking at her…his eyes filled with desire. And curiosity. Her heart thumped, the rhythm increasing when he reached out and cupped her face against his broad palm. He gently skimmed his thumb over her cheek, then leaned closer.

"There're a hundred things I want to ask you, want to know about you," he said, his voice low and husky. "But I can't wait any longer for this..."

His lips brushed over hers once, twice, with light, searching, experimental strokes that left her breathless for more, and straining closer to him. He slid his arm around her waist, drawing her nearer, and she went willingly, twining her arms around his neck. His mouth, that lovely mouth, slanted across hers, and with a deep, pleasurable sigh, she parted her lips and invited him to explore.

An appreciative *mmm* echoed through her mind. He tasted delicious. Like warm man and cool wine. His tongue danced seductively, slowly with hers, causing the most delightful friction that ignited all her dormant nerve endings. There was nothing hurried in his kiss—rather, he devastated her with his complete lack of haste, as if he intended to take hours to savor her, learn her. He slowly caressed her back, his fingertips teasing her sensitive nape, shooting a cascade of delightful shivers down her spine. His scent—a crisp, clean, masculine fragrance—surrounded her, filling her with the desire to bury her face against his neck and simply breathe him in.

Her hand sifted into his thick, silky hair. Then her fingers trailed down the strong column of his throat to slip beneath his collar. His pulse thumped hard and fast against her fingers, and she thrilled that he clearly found their kiss as arousing as she. She didn't know what to do—strain closer to him, or melt into an overcooked noodlelike heap.

Slowly he leaned back, ending their kiss, and Riley forced her eyes open. He looked at her with a glazed expression that she knew had to match her own.

"Wow," she said, in a smoky voice she didn't recognize.

"Ditto," he said, not too steadily. "That was...what was that? Incredible seems a good place to start, but somehow, it doesn't seem to do it justice."

"I think my insides...imploded. Then turned to syrup."

He bent his head and touched his lips to the tender skin just below her ear. "Syrup," he repeated softly, his breath tickling across her ear, eliciting another swirl of desire. "You know how I like sweet stuff."

She leaned back in the circle of his arms, smiled, and mentally chalked up another plus in the pro column—the man definitely knew how to kiss. "You have a gorgeous mouth. And you know how to use it."

"Thank you. You and your gorgeous mouth inspired me."

"And you're inspiring me to forget that I know next to nothing about you." While she was fully ready to embrace her long-suppressed inner devil, she had no intention of being irresponsible. "Even though I'm happy to report that I can now add incredible kisser to my short list of knowledge, I need to know more before we take this to the next step." Easing away until she'd put a bit of space between them, she picked up her wineglass and took a soothing, cool sip.

He spread his hands. "Ask me anything. I'm an open book."

"Your name is probably a good place to start," she

said with a smile. "And where you live, what you do for a living, if there are any outstanding warrants for your arrest. You know, the basics."

He laughed. "We skipped that part, didn't we? Well, there're no outstanding warrants. Closest I've ever come to trouble with the law was a speeding ticket when I was nineteen. I live in New York and work for Prestige Residential Construction, who sponsored the carnival where I encountered Madame Sees-All."

"You're kidding! *I* work for Prestige here in Atlanta," Riley said, smiling in amazement.

There was no mistaking his pleased surprise. "Small world." He held out his hand. "I'm Jackson Lange."

Riley froze. Then she felt her smile slowly fade. Everything inside her cringed with a heartfelt *nooooo*. There was no way this man could be the odious Barracuda Lange.

"Uh-oh," he said, his smile turning lopsided. "Based on your expression, it looks like my reputation preceded me." He held up his hands in mock surrender. "All lies. None of it true. I'm a nice guy. Ask my mom."

"Not necessary. I already know what kind of guy you are." She eased herself farther away from him, then pinned him with a frosty glare. "I'm Riley Addison."

If she'd been capable of laughter, she would have chuckled at his dumbfounded expression. "You. Are. Not."

"You want to see ID?"

He shook his head, then dragged a hand through his hair, staring at her as if she'd just sprouted another head. Silence stretched between them.

Finally she asked, "What are you doing in Atlanta?"

"Marcus invited me for the weekend. Wanted me to check out tonight's carnival, have dinner together tomorrow night, then visit the Atlanta offices on Monday."

Riley suppressed a groan. If he was having dinner with Marcus tomorrow, that meant he'd be attending the lake house gathering. Great.

His gaze searched her face, and then he shook his head, his eyes filled with stunned disbelief. "You're not at all what I imagined."

"Neither are you. I envisioned you with a beer belly, yellow teeth, nose and ear hair and a bad combover. Sort of an uglier version of Austin Powers."

"Gee, thanks. Although I can't really be too insulted since I envisioned you with a pinched face, no teeth, gray hair in a severe bun, and a fondness for the sort of shoes prison wardens wear. Sort of an uglier version of the Wicked Witch of the West." His gaze narrowed. "You've made my job very difficult since the day I started."

"And I suppose you think you've been a delight? Since the day you started with Prestige, my stress levels have hit Everest heights."

"They wouldn't if you'd just cooperate, instead of fighting me every step of the way."

"I'd be much more inclined to cooperate if you didn't make outrageous demands and expect instantaneous results. You seem to think I should mail you a blank company check."

"And you seem to think that I can spearhead a new marketing campaign to entice Elite Builders to the bargaining table on a shoestring budget. Are you always so tightfisted—or is it just with me?"

"Are you always so demanding and arrogant—or just with me?"

"If I'm demanding it's because I'm working with too little money and very tight time constraints."

"So is everyone else. They manage to play nicely with others. I never had a problem working with Bob Wright, the previous head of marketing."

"I'm not Bob Wright."

"Sad, but true."

"Nor am I arrogant."

An unladylike snort escaped Riley. "You don't think so? How would you describe yourself?"

"Determined. Ambitious. Confident."

"Yes, well, you say *tomayto*, I say *tomahto*. And by the way, I'm not tightfisted. I'm fiscally responsible."

"Nooo. You're fiscally anal retentive. There's a difference. Did you look over the new budget spreadsheet I e-mailed you yesterday?"

"Yes. The answer is no."

"'No' to what part of it?"

"All of it. It's ridiculous to think I'd put through a budget where all you did was double all of last year's numbers. I need detailed support and explanations for those increases. The budget I worked out with Bob stands."

"That's simply unacceptable. The department's needs have drastically changed. The budget needs to reflect that. You can't just refuse my request out of hand."

"I can, and I have." She leaned forward and glared at him. "I'll tell you what—you send me a reasonable request, one that isn't for a one-hundred-percent increase across the board, and I'll give it the time and consideration it deserves."

He imitated her gesture and leaned closer to her. "Just double the budget. I'll give back any surplus."

Riley stared at him, then shook her head. "It's actually scary because I can see that you're serious."

"I am. It wouldn't have been an issue at my last firm."

"Then how unfortunate for all of us that you didn't stay at that firm. My department doesn't work that way."

"Can't we reach a compromise on the budget I already sent you? I don't have the time to delve into the minutia of every projected expense down to the penny."

"That's too bad—for you. I can't compromise on nebulous figures you've pulled out of a hat. This isn't a flea market where we bargain—where you ask for a thousand, I counteroffer five hundred and we meet somewhere in the middle. I need hard, supported dollar amounts."

"And I need a budget increase. Five minutes ago."

"Speaking of five minutes ago, that's when I should have left here."

She scooted toward the end of the curved bench, but halted when he laid his hand on her forearm. "Riley, wait."

Flicking her gaze down to his large hand, she gritted her teeth in annoyance when a warm tingle eased through her. Her mental list showed an impressive number of items in the pro column, but the one item in the con column blew them all out of the water—this man was Jackson Lange. That ended all discussion.

Unfortunately, her hormones hadn't gotten the message. Her mind knew Jackson Lange was the last guy on earth she wanted to be around, but her long-denied and thoroughly aroused body hadn't yet fallen in with the program.

"Wait for what?" she asked. "You have my answer. Besides, I'm officially off the clock. Office hours start again at 9:00 a.m. Monday morning. I don't want to talk about work until then."

"Then let's not talk about work."

Something in his voice stilled her and she looked at him carefully. He regarded her with an expression she couldn't decipher, but even so, a ripple of awareness shivered down her spine.

"What else would we talk about?" she asked slowly, somehow feeling as if she were navigating a mine field.

"Anything. We didn't lack for conversation before we introduced ourselves."

"That's right. And that's because we *hadn't* introduced ourselves. If I'd known you were Jackson Lange, believe me, your palm reading would have gone down much differently."

What looked like reluctant humor kindled in his eyes. "Yeah, I can just imagine what sort of dire, grisly future you would have predicted for me. Still, you can't deny that up until a few minutes ago, we'd really hit it off."

"*Physically*, I suppose we did," her conscience made her admit.

"You *suppose* we did? There's no 'suppose' about it. You felt the same spark I did."

Spark? More like electrocution. "Fine. I felt it. But *felt* is the operative word."

"I disagree."

"Not a surprise, since we've disagreed about everything since Day One."

"This has nothing to do with work." His gaze

searched hers, then he asked, "So what do we do now?"

Her brows shot up. "*Now?* Are you kidding? I'm outta here."

"So you don't want to see where that kiss would lead?"

That stopped her and she cursed whatever rotten luck had made this man—this gorgeous man who had her motor humming and her cylinders popping—turn out to be Jackson Lange. Yes, she wanted to know where that kiss would lead...but not with him.

Still, she found herself asking, "I take it that you want to know?"

His gaze dropped to her lips and she felt his heated look like a caress. When his eyes again met hers, he said, "Yes, I do. I'm not happy about it, but I can't deny that I want to see where it would lead." Clearly her expression indicated that he was being less than honest because he added, "Whatever else you may think of me, I'm not a liar. I was attracted to you the minute I saw you. Even though I wish it otherwise, I still am. My mind knows you're Riley Addison, Public Enemy Number One, but I'm afraid my body hasn't fallen into line yet."

She blinked. His words so closely mirrored her own thoughts. Humph. In light of his honesty, she supposed she'd have to be honest as well. Drawing a deep breath, she said, "Listen, I know exactly where that kiss would lead. To disaster."

"Why disaster?"

"You even need to ask? We're like oil and water. We work for the same company. In feuding departments. We don't like each other. As I'm sure you're aware, you have a reputation as a barracuda, and

frankly that's a trait I don't admire. Further intimacies would make an already difficult working relationship even more impossible."

Something flickered in his eyes. "I don't know
what it's like here in Atlanta, but in New York, being
regarded as a 'barracuda' is a necessity to survive in
the cutthroat job market. And for your information,
I also have a reputation as a hard worker and a
stand-up guy. There's nothing wrong with ambition
and wanting to get to the top."

"There is if you stomp on people to get there."

"What are you talking about? I don't play dirty
and I haven't stomped on anyone. Ever."

"There were a number of talented Prestige employees who could have, *should* have been promoted
to the position you swooped into."

"Lucky for me that wasn't your decision to
make," he shot back. "Just because I was hired from
the outside doesn't mean I stomped on anyone."

Riley had to admit, albeit grudgingly, that he was
right. And that just irked her more.

Before she could say anything else, he said, "You
realize that we would be sharing all sorts of those
'further intimacies' you mentioned right now if my
name had been John Smith."

As much as she wanted to deny it, her pesky conscience wouldn't let her. "Most likely," she agreed.
"But your name isn't John Smith. Us sleeping together is a recipe that starts with 'bubble, bubble, toil
and trouble.'"

His hand skimmed down her arm, then he inter-
twined their fingers. Riley shot an inward frown at
her ridiculously overactive hormones. *This is not the
guy to get all in an uproar over,* she told her hormones
firmly. *He is not going to light your fuse. Go back to sleep.*

"I'm willing to forget your name if you'll forget mine," he said softly, his fingers brushing lightly over hers.

She shook her head. "All flames were extinguished when you uttered the name Jackson Lange." *If only.*

"Your racing pulse and the desire in your eyes say differently."

She pulled her hand away. "If my pulse is fast it's only because I'm annoyed."

"I'm not thrilled, either. But this isn't the office and we're not at work. Right now all I see is a beautiful woman wearing a sexy red dress who I'd like to get to know better. And I can only figure that the reason you came here was to get to know me better."

"And I have. I found out that I'm positive that this would not work out at all. Ever." She slid from the booth and stood. He made a move to rise, but she held out her hand. "Please don't get up." She met his gaze squarely and once again cursed the fact that he was who he was. "I'm going home. I'm going to forget this ever happened. I suggest you do the same."

Without giving him an opportunity to reply, she quickly exited the bar, then strode across the lobby where she presented her ticket to the bellman at the valet desk. She didn't draw an easy breath until she'd fastened her seat belt and exited the hotel parking lot.

Good Lord, what a disaster. Not to mention a disappointment. If bad luck were an Olympic event, she would have brought home the gold tonight. Just when she'd been totally primed to emerge from her cocoon, just when she'd met a man who interested her—a man who'd fired up her libido with a blaze of hunger like no other man ever had—what happens? He turns out to be her nemesis.

A nemesis who'd attracted her like bees to honey. Who'd kissed her until she couldn't feel her knees. Who clearly had wanted to set aside their work differences and just concentrate on the palpable attraction they'd both felt.

If only it were that easy.

If only his name *had* been John Smith.

If only she didn't have to see him again tomorrow at Marcus's house.

Had she actually told him she was going to forget this ever happened? A great plan. But the fact that her lips still tingled, that the delicious taste of him still lingered on her tongue, gave rise to the sneaking suspicion that it would take a long, long time to forget their kiss. The way his hands had felt brushing over her skin. The sensation of his strong arms wrapped around her. The press of his thigh against hers. The heated arousal in his eyes and all it had promised.

Damn. This was suddenly turning into a very long weekend.

THE NEXT AFTERNOON, Riley leaned against the railing of Marcus Thornton's spacious deck and admired the spectacular view of Lake Lanier. Built at the point of a secluded cove, the house offered unimpeded vistas of the sparkling blue-green waters of the expansive lake. Colorful sails dotted the horizon, along with houseboats, cruisers, outboards and Jet Skis. Her gaze shifted to the shaded trail below which led from the lower level of the house to the boat dock where an outboard and a Jet Ski bobbed gently in the water.

With her eyes shaded by her dark sunglasses, she surreptitiously checked out the group standing on the dock, chatting, enjoying the sunshine; Marcus, holding a frosted beer mug, his distinguished gray hair covered by a baseball hat emblazoned with the Prestige logo. Prestige CFO Paul Stanfield, indulging in a cigar, nodding at whatever Marcus was saying.

And Jackson Lange.

Casually dressed in a short-sleeve yellow Polo shirt tucked into cream khakis, his dark hair gleaming in the sunlight, he looked tall, masculine, and good enough to nibble on. A long-neck beer bottle dangled casually from his fingers and she instantly recalled the feel of those talented fingers skimming over her neck. A whoosh of heat that had nothing to do with the eighty-five-degree temperature sizzled through her. Pulling her gaze away from the trio, she walked to the cooler resting in a shady corner of the deck to grab an icy soft drink.

No sooner had she popped the top than Gloria stepped out onto the deck. The instant Gloria saw her, she made a beeline toward Riley.

"You look like an ad for a fabulous tropical vacation," Riley said admiring her friend's bright orange sundress decorated with splashes of yellow, lime and turquoise.

"Thank you. You look pretty spiffy yourself," Gloria said, her gaze taking in Riley's aqua sundress that hugged her upper body before flaring into a full skirt that brushed just above her knees. "That color is great on you."

"Thanks." Riley decided not to share the fact that she'd changed her outfit a dozen times before leaving the house.

Gloria glanced around to make certain they were alone, then edged her designer sunglasses down her nose and peered at Riley over the rims. "Well?"

"Well, what?" Riley returned in her most innocent voice.

Gloria's eyes narrowed. "I picked up the phone to call you about ten times this morning to find out what happened last night, but on the off chance that you were still occupied with Mr. Gorgeous, I resisted. As your best friend I demand details."

Riley pinched the bridge of her nose and shook her head. "You won't believe what happened."

Concern flooded Gloria's eyes and she laid her hand on Riley's arm. "Nothing bad, I hope."

"No, no, nothing like that. But the evening took a very…unexpected turn."

"Good unexpected or bad?"

"Unbelievable unexpected."

"I'll believe it. Tell me."

"Turns out Mr. Gorgeous is none other than Jackson Lange."

Gloria blinked. "I don't believe it."

A humorless sound escaped Riley. "Told you. Unfortunately it's true. Marcus invited him to Atlanta for the weekend and he decided to check out the carnival. Even worse, we didn't exchange names until after we'd kissed." Her traitorous lips tingled in remembrance of his mouth and tongue exploring hers.

A noise that sounded suspiciously like a smothered laugh came from Gloria. "I know it isn't funny, but Lord, Riley, this could only happen to you." Gloria's gaze turned speculative. "So how was the kiss?"

Riley shrugged. "Nice." Her conscience slapped her for the lukewarm word and she shooed the pesky inner voice away.

"Just 'nice'?"

"My enthusiasm was pretty much doused when he told me his name."

"So I take it you didn't sleep with him."

"Hardly. I couldn't wait to escape." She blew out a long breath. "And to top it all off, he's *here*." She jerked her head toward the lake. "Down at the boat dock with Marcus and Paul."

"Really?" Gloria immediately walked to the railing and pretended to admire the lake views. Riley joined her and noted that the three men were making their way back to the house.

"Oh, my," Gloria said. "If he looks that good at a distance, I can only imagine he's quite...potent up close. Have you spoken to him yet?"

"No. He was down at the dock with Marcus and Paul when I arrived. But I'm prepared to face him. I mean, it's not like the flirting or the kiss were any big deal."

"Hmm. Okay."

"It's not as if I won't find some other guy to light my fuse."

"You bet."

"It's not like we ever have to mention last night again."

"Right."

"It's not as if we can't forget about it."

"If you say so."

"Or that it would ever happen again."

Gloria raised her brows. "Are you trying to convince me—or yourself?"

"I'm not trying to convince anyone. I'm just stating the facts. Where Jackson Lange is concerned, I'm going to strictly adhere to Plan A—be cordial, make small talk if needed, then stay as far away from him as possible. I'll just pretend that he's not here."

Gloria glanced over the railing at the approaching men. She expelled a dreamy-sounding sigh, then patted Riley's hand. "I wish you luck with that, Riley. I really do. But I think you'd better come up with a Plan B because that yummy man is not going to be easy to ignore."

3

JACKSON LEANED against the deck rail with a noncha-
lance he was far from feeling. He stood amongst a
group of a half-dozen Prestige employees, and sent
up a silent thank-you that someone else was carrying
the conversational ball so he wasn't required to do
more than nod or shake his head. Because in truth, he
had no clue what the hell they were talking about.
Was it sports? Stocks? The weather? Who the hell
knew? Not him, that was for sure. And it was all *her*
fault.

She hadn't been out of his thoughts from the moment he'd laid eyes on her. He'd spent a sleepless
night, alternately tossing and turning, staring at the
ceiling, his mind replaying every second of their
meeting, then torturing himself with fantasies of
what might have been.

And now he found himself trying to think of the
last time he'd been so painfully aware of a woman—
and came up blank. Other than exchanging a few polite words when he'd returned from the boat dock,
they hadn't spoken. But he'd known where she was
every second.

She looked...incredible. Trim and fit in a sleeveless dress the color of a tropical sea that left her
golden tanned shoulders bare, a tantalizing treat that
beckoned him to touch. She stood on the opposite

side of the deck, chatting and smiling with a group of two men and three women. To the best of his knowledge, she hadn't so much as glanced in his direction the entire afternoon, a fact that irked him since he couldn't seem to tear his gaze away from her. Only his dark-lensed Ray-Bans kept his fascination with her a secret from the other guests.

He lifted his cola to his lips and gave himself a mental shake. What the hell was it about this woman that had him so thrown off-kilter? Yes, she was attractive, but so were a lot of women. Yet, for reasons he couldn't explain, he'd taken one look at her last night and *pow*—direct hit to the solar plexus. Unfortunately her impact was no less overwhelming today. It was as if she exuded some sort of feminine force field that drew him like steel to a magnet. And while she'd clearly put last night's encounter and their kiss out of her mind, he'd been spectacularly unsuccessful doing so—another fact that seriously irked him.

Damn. Why, out of all the women he encountered, did the one who hit him like a lightning bolt have to be Riley Addison? And why hadn't the fact that this woman made his life miserable turn him off? Or that she'd referred to him as a barracuda—something else which really rankled.

He knew the frustration of being passed over for a promotion he'd worked his ass off to earn—had learned that tough lesson at his very first job out of college. He'd sworn right then he'd never let that happen again. He loved the challenge of marketing and he was determined to succeed. He wanted to establish himself to secure his future, provide a stable life for himself and the family he hoped to someday have. Manhattan was tough, but he'd risen to the challenge. But he'd earned everything he'd ever achieved—with his integrity intact. So why should he care what Riley Addison thought? He shouldn't.

But damn it, he did.

Obviously his recent sexual drought was having a hugely detrimental effect on him, leaving him unable to channel his desires toward an appropriate partner. Desiring Riley Addison was unsuitable and unwanted in so many ways, it didn't even bear considering. But there was simply no talking his body out of it. Double damn.

"How about I fire up the outboard?" Marcus suggested, jerking Jackson from his thoughts. "Who's up for a little waterskiing?"

Of the dozen guests, half of them assented. Riley wasn't one of them, Jackson noted, but the woman she'd been talking to most of the afternoon, an attractive redhead named Gloria who headed up Prestige's IT department, said, "I want to ski."

"The rest of you can take turns with the Jet Ski, then we'll switch." He shot a grin across the deck. "Riley, as I recall from last year, you chickened out. I also recall you promising you'd try it next year—which, as it happens, turns out to be this year."

"I didn't chicken out, I simply didn't know how to operate a Jet Ski," Riley said with a smile. "Unfortunately, I still don't."

"Not a problem. The model I just bought seats two. All you need is a driver and some arms to hold on. Since you've got arms…" Marcus turned and pinned his gaze on Jackson. "Let's give the new guy first crack. You know how to drive a Jet Ski?"

"As a matter of fact, I do."

"Great." He turned back to Riley, his smile filled with the same challenge that Jackson imagined was a big part of the CEO's business success. "All settled. Jackson will take you for a ride."

Riley's head whipped around to stare at Jackson—at least, he assumed she was looking at him. Impossible to tell with her sunglasses. But the fact that she looked seriously displeased was a big hint that she was glaring at him.

Well, good. Why should he be the only one feeling unsettled? Buoyed by the fact that her neat feathers were obviously ruffled, he strolled over to her, his heart thumping ridiculously at the prospect of having her hold onto him for dear life. It was an opportunity he sure as hell wasn't going to pass up.

"Looks like it's you and me, Riley. On the Jet Ski." He grinned. "How's that for a poem?"

"I've heard better. And as for the Jet Ski, thanks, but I'll pass." She turned toward her friend. "Gloria, weren't you just saying that you wanted to try it out?" Jackson was certain he detected a note of desperation in her voice.

Gloria shook her head. "I'm with the waterskiing group. Gotta go change into my bathing suit." She smiled, waggled her fingers, then entered the house through the sliding screen doors.

Jackson made a tsking sound. "I'm surprised. I wouldn't have taken you for a..." He flapped his arms and made chicken noises.

She lifted her chin. "I am *not* a chicken."

"Do you know how to swim?"

"Of course."

"Then what's the problem?"

"Maybe I just don't want to ride on a Jet Ski with *you*."

He studied her for several seconds, then leaned forward so no one could overhear. "Liar. You want to just as much as I do."

"You really are very arrogant."

"No. I'm just not afraid to be honest."

"Neither am I. So here's the unvarnished truth— I don't relish the thought of you being in charge while I'm relegated to the role of passenger."

"I'm not surprised. You're clearly one of those 'I must be in charge at all times' types."

"Wrong. I'm simply very particular about who I hand over the reins to, especially with something like this. I'm not all that fond of water sports."

"Why not?"

"I broke my arm waterskiing when I was ten. I much prefer land sports. Like baseball."

"Baseball." He shook his head. "Again, I'm not surprised that your favorite sport is one that's overly organized to the point where the excitement is non-existent."

He could feel her glare through her sunglasses. "Is that a not-so-subtle way to imply I'm boring?"

"*I'm* not the one afraid to ride the Jet Ski. Now me, I'm a tennis fan—a fast-moving game where you roll with the punches."

"Uh-huh. Where the players never get dirty and spend hours swatting at little fuzzy yellow balls."

Her gaze shifted with unmistakable trepidation to the dock where the Jet Ski bobbed in the water, and guilt nibbled at Jackson for baiting her. "Listen, since you're obviously nervous—"

"I'm not nervous. Exactly." She bit her lower lip, drawing Jackson's attention to her lush mouth. "I don't think Jet Skis are unsafe. It's just that one Jet Ski plus my luck multiplied by my lack of coordination is an equation that doesn't add up for me."

"I see. Well, in that case, I'll take it as slow as you want to go."

The speed with which she swiveled her attention back to him offered all the proof he needed that she felt the same sizzling awareness that was nearly suffocating him. Clearly all her nervousness wasn't due solely to the Jet Ski. He moved a step closer to her and noted with satisfaction that her breath hitched. Definitely not as calm and collected as she wanted him to believe. Excellent.

"You just tell me how fast, or how slow, you want me to go, Riley," he said softly, "and I'll be happy to oblige you."

Color rose in her cheeks, and he heard her swallow. Her lips parted slightly and a vivid memory of their heated kiss slammed into him. "Are we still talking about the Jet Ski?" she asked, her voice slightly breathless.

No. "Of course."

She licked her lips. "You know, as an accountant, I'm a numbers sort of gal, and ever since I broke my arm waterskiing, the water sport numbers just don't add up for me."

"What water sport numbers?"

"One minute on a Jet Ski, two seconds of uncoordination, three dozen injuries, ten years of traumatic post-ride nightmares…" She shook her head. "The debits just don't equal the credits."

"But you haven't added everything into the equation. How about the satisfaction of saying, 'I did it, I'm not a chicken—so there' to Marcus."

"Hmm. That *is* tempting."

"And of course, the satisfaction of saying the same thing to me."

"*Extremely* tempting." She expelled a long breath. "You won't go jumping over any waves?"

"Not unless you want me to." He raised his right hand. "Scout's promise."

"Ha. You don't strike me as the Boy Scout type."

"You'd be wrong. I was a Scout for seven years."

"That was a loooooong time ago."

"Maybe, but even former Scouts still get to use the promise. So, what's it going to be? Are you up for the challenge? Or are you going to wimp out, thus enabling me to lord your great display of chickenish behavior over your head for the next fifty years or so?"

"You'd do that, too, wouldn't you." It was a statement rather than a question, and issued in a clearly disgruntled tone.

He smiled. "In a New York minute."

"You know, you're really very annoying."

"At last, a meeting of the minds. To Jet Ski, or not to Jet Ski, that is the question." He inclined his head. "And your answer is…?"

She pressed her lips together and he had to fight to keep a straight face. She so obviously didn't want to go, yet she also clearly balked at throwing in the towel. Finally she said, "Fine. I'll go. But if you go fast, I'm going to grab hold of your earlobes and pull until I can tie them under your chin like bonnet strings."

"Not a fashion look I'm overly fond of."

"Then we understand each other."

"In regards to the Jet Ski, yes."

"I suppose that the sooner we get going, the sooner the torture will end."

Instead of feeling insulted, he couldn't help but laugh at her disgruntled tone. "That's the spirit."

"I'll go change."

"Me, too. Meet you on the dock in ten minutes."

She muttered something under her breath that sounded suspiciously like she'd rather *deck* him in ten minutes, then she entered the house looking seriously displeased. Jackson chuckled. He should probably be ashamed of himself for baiting her, but he wasn't. This afternoon was turning out to be a lot more fun than he'd expected. And there was no denying the anticipation he was feeling at the thought of having her wrapped around him on that Jet Ski.

Ten minutes later, he stood on the dock with the gathering group of water-skiers. There was much commotion and laughter as everyone settled themselves in the boat, and Jackson accepted the Jet Ski keys and two orange life vests from Marcus. He'd just slipped his arms into the vest when he caught sight of Riley approaching the dock. His fingers stilled on the zipper as he tried, and failed, not to stare.

She wore a simple, bright yellow two-piece bathing suit that looked like a tank top paired with a bikini bottom. The suit exposed an inch of toned abdomen—a tantalizing, teasing glimpse he found far sexier than any more revealing swimsuit he'd ever seen.

His gaze traveled downward, taking in the matching short mesh skirt, tied sarong-style around her hips, that showcased long, trim legs with each fluid step. Neon green-and-yellow flip-flops adorned her feet.

She continued toward him, and he clenched his jaw so his mouth wouldn't flop open. Damn. The way the woman *walked* turned him on. And he couldn't explain why. There was nothing overtly sexy about her bathing suit or the way she moved. But even though he couldn't explain it, he sure as hell couldn't deny the heat she inspired in him.

Forcing himself from his stupor, he concentrated on zipping up his life jacket. When she stepped onto the dock, he handed her a vest. "All set?" he asked.

"Ready as I'll ever be." The way she glanced at the Jet Ski told him she really was nervous about this, and his conscience kicked him for teasing her.

Stepping closer, he said in an undertone so only she could hear, "Listen, if you're really worried, we don't have to do this."

Skepticism was written all over her face. "Oh, you'd just love that."

"I'm serious. I'll delay the proceedings until Marcus leaves with the boat, then we'll just head back up to the deck."

She looked at him, and for what felt like the hundredth time today, he cursed the sunglasses that hid her eyes. "A chivalrous offer," she finally said, "but I'm determined to give this a try—if for no other reason than to see if you're a man of your word."

"Meaning?"

"I want to see if you'll really go as slow, or fast, as I want."

He tamped back the erotic images her words sent ricocheting through his mind and forced a smile. "It will be my pleasure to dispel your doubts regarding my integrity. And I'm sure you didn't mean to sound so shocked that I'd make a chivalrous gesture."

"Oh, believe me, I'm shocked."

"Then be prepared for another shock." He stepped back and extended his hand toward the Jet Ski. "Ladies first. See? I'm just full of good manners."

"Yes, you're just full of it, all right." She shot him a sweet smile, then walked toward the end of the dock while pulling on her life vest. Jackson followed her, and even though he tried not to, he couldn't stop himself from checking out the rear view. And damn, what a fine view it was.

"I'll get on first," Jackson said, "so I can help you on board." After he'd settled himself on the sun-warmed seat, he extended his hand to Riley. She drew what appeared to be a bracing breath, then slipped her hand into his. Their palms met and Jackson's fingers gripped hers in a steady hold, as heat radiated up his arm. She carefully stepped onto the craft, then straddled the seat behind him.

Jackson went totally still at the sensation of her smooth inner thighs cradling his legs. Blood rushed to his groin, and he shifted a bit, relieved that his sitting position camouflaged his budding erection. Then she scooted closer to him and he winced at his body's swift reaction.

She slipped her arms around him and he looked down to see that her fingers were clenched around his life vest in a white-knuckle grip.

"I don't mind if you hold on, but you're cutting off my air supply," he said over his shoulder.

"Just want to be prepared in case we take a freak-ish bounce. I don't want to fall off this thing."

"Not much chance of that, what with the strong-hold you have going there."

"Hey, if I fall off, your torso is going with me."

"I believe it. And I'm not much comforted by that. Just try not to crack my ribs, okay?"

"Don't go fast and I won't have any reason to."

Just then, Marcus and crew cast off from the dock. "Have fun," he called while everyone waved. Jackson returned their wave, then grunted when Riley's arms tightened around his middle.

"Keep both hands on the handlebars—or whatever you call the steering apparatus—at all times, Captain."

If he'd been able to draw a deep enough breath, he would have laughed. "Riley. I haven't even started the engine yet."

Her grip relaxed enough for him to breathe. "Oh. Well, get to it so we can get this over with. We haven't even left the dock and already it feels like I've been sitting on this thing for three days."

Chuckling, he inserted the key and started the engine. After a few revs, he released the ropes mooring them to the dock, then pushed them off. Instead of heading toward the open lake, he turned into the cove.

"Whoa, speed demon—how fast are you going?" she shouted directly into his ear over the hum of the motor.

"About three miles an hour. We could swim faster than this. If I go any slower, the engine will stall. And Riley—easy on the eardrums, okay?"

"First the ribs, now the eardrums—has anyone ever told you that you're very fussy?"

"No. So what does that tell you?"

A long sigh brushed past his ear, shooting another bolt of heat through him. "Sorry. I didn't mean to squeeze you or take out your eardrum. I'm just a little nervous."

"Really? I hadn't noticed," he teased.

"Ha, ha."

"There's nothing to be nervous about. This isn't so terrible, is it?"

"Well…I suppose it's okay—so far. Where are we going?"

"For now, just to the end of the cove. We can check out the other houses, and it will give you a chance to relax. Once you've gotten the feel of it, if you decide you like it, we can head out into the lake."

Riley drew in a shaky breath and swallowed hard to resettle her heart back where it belonged. Had he just said "once you've gotten the feel of it?" "If you decide you like it?" Much as it bugged her to admit it, she'd gotten the feel of it the instant she'd sat down—the feel of her thighs straddling his muscular legs, the dark, masculine hair tickling her skin. The sensation of her arms wrapped around him in a way that made her want to strip off his life vest so she could hug his bare torso, feel his skin beneath her fingertips, and explore all those lovely contours she'd caught a glimpse of before he'd zipped up the vest. The sunshine glinting off his windblown dark hair, beckoning her fingers to ruffle the mussed strands. The crisp, clean scent wafting off his skin, filling her with the desire to lean forward and bury her nose against the strong column of his neck. And the sight of his muscular arms gripping the handles.

He thought she was gripping him so tightly because she feared falling off the Jet Ski, but that was only partially true. In truth, she had to hold on tight to keep herself from giving in to the temptation to skim her palms down those lovely, muscular arms to test their strength.

Oh, yeah, she'd gotten the feel of it all right.

And it had taken all of two seconds to decide she liked it.

Her nervousness over riding the Jet Ski—a feeling she'd clung to like a lifeline—was retreating at an alarming rate, drowned out by the almost painful sexual awareness she'd tried so hard all afternoon to suppress. If it had been any other man than Jackson Lange eliciting this response in her, she would have turned cartwheels. She'd wanted an adventure, wanted to soar, but not with Jackson Lange.

Well, okay, she *wanted* to—desperately. But damn it, she didn't *want* to want to. And the fact that he'd been so decent about her apprehension made him, well...sort of likable. Damn.

They chugged slowly along, and bit by bit, Riley's apprehension eased. The homes along the lake were beautiful, and by the time they reached the end of the cove where Jackson navigated a wide turn, she was feeling pretty seaworthy.

"Hey, you can crank it up to five miles an hour, Captain."

He turned and grinned at her over his shoulder, setting her pulse to "flutter." "As you wish, oh most brave First Mate."

He adjusted their speed. A few minutes later, as they neared the Thornton dock, he said, "Want to quit, or you want to see what this bad boy can do?"

A loaded question if she'd ever heard one. And God help her, she *so* wanted to know. But surely he was referring to the Jet Ski—wasn't he? "You *swear* you know how to handle this thing?"

"Sweetheart, I grew up on the water and started driving the family Jet Ski when I was twelve. You're in very capable hands."

A bonfire of heat erupted on her skin at the unwanted sensual images *that* comment evoked. Even though she hated to admit it, she was nowhere near ready for this ride to end. This Jackson Lange seemed very different from the man who fired off terse, demanding e-mails. This Jackson Lange inspired confidence, and inspired her to be brave. To take chances.

"All right. Let's see what this bad boy can do."

He turned and grinned. "Atta girl. You're in for the ride of your life."

He punched up their speed a bit and headed for the open lake. Riley tightened her grip on his life vest and felt him laugh. When they reached the end of the cove, he accelerated, and in an instant it seemed as if they were flying across the water. At first, she couldn't catch her breath, but soon the sheer exhilaration of the speed, the rush of warm air whipping wildly through her hair and the spray of lake water cooling her sun-heated skin all conspired to invigorate her and chase away the last remnants of her apprehension.

Jackson was true to his word, and clearly knew how to handle the craft with a deft hand. She clung to him as they jumped the wakes of outboards and cruisers. Soon Riley found herself laughing as if she were on an amusement-park ride, and yelled, "Again! Faster!"

Jackson obliged her, and they dashed along, like a motorized porpoise, skipping over the waves. After another few jumps, Jackson yelled over his shoulder, "Want to take a breather and check out one of these little islands?"

Since a breather sounded good, she yelled back, "Sure."

He turned the Jet Ski toward one of the many little heavily treed islands that dotted the lake, providing boaters with anchorages, shady picnic havens and tiny beaches. As they approached the strip of a sandy beach, Jackson slowed the Jet Ski, then killed the engine. He eased off the seat, then, with the water up to his knees, he towed the craft to the beach. When the bottom scraped the sand, he offered his hand to Riley.

"All ashore who's going ashore," he said with a smile.

Riley slipped off her flip-flops, then accepted his hand, stepping down onto the coarse sand. Cool water lapped at her ankles, and she helped Jackson pull the Jet Ski farther up onto the beach.

When they finished, he grinned at her from across the Jet Ski. "Well?"

She smiled in return, then heaved out an exaggerated sigh. "Fine. Never let it be said that I can't admit when I'm wrong—and I was wrong. That was terrific. Completely…"

Her voice trailed off and she stared. As she'd spoken, he'd unzipped his vest. When he'd slipped it off his shoulders and laid it across the vinyl seat, every thought drained from her head, except the one that whispered *whoooooeeeee.*

Why he was a marketing executive instead of an underwear model she couldn't imagine, because he put those Calvin Klein guys to shame. Wide shoulders gave way to a well-defined chest and abs. The dark hair accenting his broad chest narrowed to a ribbon that disappeared into the waistband of his dark blue swim trunks—a silky, midnight trail that tempted her to trace it to its end…with her tongue. He was beautiful in clothes, but good Lord, in swim trunks he was stupendous. She could only imagine that he'd be utterly heart-stopping without any clothes at all.

He rested his hands on his hips, and her gaze riveted on his splayed fingers that seemed to point directly to his groin like flashing neon arrows. Desire ignited with a flash of heat so intense it felt as if the sun had just moved closer to the earth.

"Completely what?" he asked, yanking her attention—and her wayward gaze—away from his fascinating groin.

She blinked, then said the only thing she could think of. "Huh?"

"You were waxing poetic about the ride, and my, ahem, superior handling skills, when you sort of drifted off."

A vivid image of his superior handling skills—ones that had nothing to do with Jet Skis—flashed in her mind. She swallowed and pressed her mental Rewind button to pick up the thought processes the sight of him had derailed. "Right. It was completely... incredible."

"No argument from me. And I'm glad you liked it."

Oh, yes, she'd liked it. Far more than she should have. Certainly far more than she'd wanted to. Any doubts she may have harbored about her body's reaction to Jackson were long gone. The sensation of him cradled between her thighs, her arms wrapped around him, would definitely keep her awake tonight—again.

He pushed his sunglasses up to rest on his head, then turned his attention to scanning the small island, and Riley took the opportunity to remove her own vest.

"This is great," he said, still looking around. "Quiet, shady—we've got this little beach...all to ourselves." He turned back to her, and his gaze skimmed slowly over her. There was no missing the appreciation in his gaze, or the flare of heat in his eyes. A muscle jerked in his jaw, and then he reached up for his glasses and tossed them on top of his life vest. "It's...hot. I'm going to take a swim before we start back." He jerked his head toward the water. "Care to join me?"

The way he was looking at her made her feel as if steam was emanating from her pores. Her common sense warned that being all wet with him was very unwise, but everything female in her strongly disagreed. Everything female won—hands down.

"A swim sounds great," she said, proud that her voice sounded so casual. She watched him stride quickly into the lake. When the water reached his waist, he made a shallow dive. When he resurfaced, he shook his head like dog, spraying glittering drops of water in every direction. After shooting her a thumbs-up, he struck out with strong, steady strokes parallel to the beach.

Riley took her time untying her mesh skirt, drawing deep calming breaths while she gave herself a mental pep talk, sternly reminding herself that he was Mr. Seven Hundred and Eighty-three Dollar Dinner. Mr. Double the Budget. This intense physical reaction to him was inexplicable and totally ridiculous. The way her body was carrying on, it was as if she'd never seen an attractive man before. Well, starting tomorrow, she'd concentrate all her efforts on finding a different man to put out this crazy fire he'd started in her. She could do that. No problem.

Opting to keep her sunglasses on just in case her wandering eyeballs decided not to behave, she walked into the lake. Cool water rose up her legs as she waded deeper—a welcome relief to the scorching heat, which could not be attributed just to the bright sun. When the water reached just below her breasts, she dipped her knees until she was submerged up to the chin, then let out a long sigh of relief. Five minutes later, Jackson swam up to her. In spite of the distance and pace he'd swum, he was barely winded, a testament to his obvious fitness.

He stood and raised his arms to push his dark wet hair back from his face, a motion that reheated everything in Riley that she'd thought she'd just cooled off. He was way too gorgeous, his movements way too sexy, and he was standing way too close. Or was he not standing close enough?

She straightened to her full height, then inched backed several inches. He stepped forward. "Enjoy your swim?" she asked, taking another step backward.

His gaze seemed to burn her. "Yes and no. Yes, the water felt good. No, my swim didn't produce the desired result."

"What desired result?"

"Do you really want to know?"

Self-preservation and the caution she'd cultivated for so long commanded she say no and get the hell out of there. But once again, everything feminine in her promptly drowned out self-preservation and caution.

"Yes, I want to know."

"I was hoping the physical activity would take the edge off my arousal. It didn't. And unfortunately, I'm starting to think that I could swim around this damn island a dozen times and it still wouldn't help."

Well, she had her answer, and it whipped up a tornado of lust that threatened to sweep away everything in its path, including, she feared, her common sense, which for the umpteenth time pointed out that this was the wrong man with whom to indulge in an affair. Before she could think up a reply—actually before she could think at all—he reached out and pushed her sunglasses up to rest on her head, exposing her eyes. His gaze searched hers intently, then he gave a tight nod.

"You feel it, too," he said.

She desperately wanted to deny it, but she hated to lie, especially after his bald-faced honesty. "I can't deny that I find you...attractive. But I'm not happy about it."

"Well, I find you *painfully* attractive, and I'm *really* not happy about it. I can't understand or explain why a woman I consider a dragon-breathing, tightfisted, thorn in my side has me so worked up, but there it is."

Riley raised her brows. "Gee, you sure do have a way with words. You get many dates with that sweet-talkin' thing you do?"

"I'm not a sweet-talker—"

"No kidding."

"I'm honest. I wanted you the instant I saw you in that gypsy tent, and even the fact that you turned out to be the dreaded Riley Addison hasn't changed that. It's like you exude some sort of...what are those things called?"

"Pheromones?"

"Yeah. Well, your pheromones have my hormones all out of whack. At work, we rub each other the wrong way, big time. But we're not at work. And the last thing I'm thinking about right now is the office." He stepped forward and drew her into his arms until they touched from chest to knee. Riley's hands rose by their own volition and settled on his upper arms while she drank in the delightful sensation of his body pressing against hers.

Oh, my. He wasn't kidding about being aroused.

He lowered his head slowly toward hers, and even as she lifted her face, she whispered, "This is so bad."

"Yeah? Feels pretty damn good to me."

4

JACKSON'S MOUTH CAME down on hers, hot, fierce and demanding, and Riley's insides turned to goo. Unlike last night's exchange, there was no gentle exploring here. No, this was a flash fire of heat that consumed her, dragging a moan of desperate want from her throat that vibrated from her mouth to his. His tongue stroked hers with devastating skill, while his hands molded her against him as if she were putty, which was pretty much what she felt like.

She strained closer, and his palms skimmed down her back to cup her bottom and lift her more firmly against him. He rubbed himself slowly against her, and even the cool water lapping at her chest couldn't subdue the fire pulsing through her veins. Her insides danced, and with all semblance of judgment fleeing at an alarming rate with her mounting arousal, Riley broke off their kiss.

Pressing her hands against his chest, she leaned back, putting a bit of distance between them, or at least between their upper bodies. His erection still pressed against her belly, and the heat burning in his gaze all but fried her where she stood. His breathing sounded as ragged as her own. The passion this man inspired in her simultaneously thrilled and frightened her.

After swallowing to find her voice, she said, "Oh, God. You made me bloop."

He cocked a brow. "Excuse me?

"Damn it, you made me bloop."

"And that's, um, bad?"

"Yes."

"It isn't a bad thing where I come from. Well, maybe for a guy, if he bloops too soon, but not for a woman."

She stared at him. "What are you talking about?"

"Damned if I know. What are *you* talking about?"

"*Bloop.* It's this weird feeling I get in my stomach when I'm kissed. I thought you made me bloop when you kissed me last night, but I wasn't sure. But now there's no doubt. I blooped for sure."

"So…this happens to you a lot?"

She shook her head. "No—that's just it. It's only ever happened twice before. Once when I was four-teen and Danny McGraw gave me my first kiss, and then again when my almost-fiancé kissed me. My stomach goes bloop—like that feeling when you jump off the high diving board, or as you plunge down on a roller coaster. You know, that tingling sensation that borders on…nausea."

"Nausea. Great. Listen, if you don't stop with all these compliments, I'm liable to go all to pieces."

"I meant 'good' nausea."

"I didn't know there was such a thing."

"There is. It's called bloop."

His expression cleared and his gaze dropped to her mouth. "Well, then—"

"No 'well then.' Bloop is really bad."

"You just said it was good."

"No. The only two guys who ever made me bloop both turned out to be creeps. I had to blacken Danny McGraw's eye when he refused to take his hand out of my bra cup, although how he got it in there in the first place, I'm still not sure. The guy was like a human octopus. And my almost-fiancé made me bloop until I found him making someone else bloop."

He winced. "Ouch. You actually caught them in the act?"

"Yes. Animal grunts and all. And don't think I didn't get rid of that picnic table."

"They were doing it on your *picnic table?*"

"Can you believe the nerve?"

"Very nervy," he agreed. "But what does that have to do with us?"

"Don't you see? I've had miserable luck with every guy who's ever made me bloop. And you made me bloop worse than the other two put together."

"Ever heard of 'third time's the charm'?"

"Yes, but—"

"I have a confession to make. I blooped, too."

Riley felt her eyes widen. "You mean—"

"Yup. A double bloop. Here's another confession—my stomach has blooped just from *looking* at you."

"Oh, boy. We're in trouble."

He leaned forward and lightly nibbled on her neck. "Did I mention that Trouble is my middle name?"

His tongue flicked over her earlobe and her eyes glazed over. "Um, no. But I'm rapidly starting to believe it."

"Trouble with a capital T."

"And that rhymes with B. And that stands for bloop." Even as her common sense tossed out a cursory warning, she arched her neck to give him better access and ignored her pesky inner voice. She simply couldn't resist the urge to touch him. To experience his kiss again. So, fine, maybe it wasn't the best idea, but neither was it a crime. She was so ready to be kissed and touched. It had been so long. And even longer since a kiss or touch had felt anything even close to this. The old Riley wouldn't have hesitated. And she was tired of waiting...

She glided her hands over his shoulders, then wound her arms around his neck. "Of course, I might be completely mistaken. Maybe I didn't bloop at all. Maybe we should try it again, just to make sure."

"I'm definitely all for making sure," he said, his husky words vibrating against her ear.

He kissed his way back to her lips, and the instant their mouths met, her stomach performed a diving swoop. While one of his hands slowly explored up and down her back, his other hand came forward to palm her breast. She groaned, and leaned into his hand. He teased her aroused nipple through the snug material, while his other hand slipped beneath her thigh and lifted her leg. Dizzy with arousal, Riley wrapped her calf around his hips and pressed her aching feminine flesh against his tempting hardness.

A sound that resembled a growl vibrated from him, and his hand returned to her back to draw drugging circles over her buttocks before easing beneath the elastic waistband of her bikini bottom. His fingers slid unerringly down over her bare buttocks, teasing sensitive nerve endings, gliding over her wet skin until he stroked her swollen feminine folds.

Sensation swamped her, inundating her with a luscious abandon she hadn't felt in...forever. Riley's head dropped limply back, and he feasted on her exposed neck, pressing heated nips and openmouthed kisses, then laving the tender skin with his tongue. All the while his fingers caressed her, driving her closer to the edge of an orgasm she was helpless to contain. He shifted her higher and slipped two fingers inside her, stroking her while his mouth once again claimed hers, his tongue caressing with the same tormenting rhythm as his fingers, his other hand arousing her breasts. She desperately tried to remain poised on the precipice, sustain the heady pleasure, but his relentless assault on her senses pushed her over the edge. A cry escaped her, and she shuddered, her orgasm throbbing through her, intense, consuming, stealing away everything save his magic fingers stroking her, his talented tongue tasting her.

As her tremors subsided, she fought to catch her breath. He held her tightly against him, and she could feel the hard, rapid thump of his pulse against her cheek where it rested against his neck. When she felt as if she could draw a breath without panting, she lifted her head.

Dark blue eyes regarded her with an expression she couldn't decipher, other than to know that it reflected intense arousal. Feeling the need to speak, she murmured the only word she could manage.

"Wow."

He jerked his head in a tight nod. "That sums it up pretty well." He searched her gaze. "Regrets?"

She considered for several seconds. "It probably won't make my list of 'smartest moves I've ever made,' but you, your touch, made me forget…everything. My restraint, my control. Where I am, who I'm with." And that was something she hadn't counted on. She'd wanted to toss off her conservative shroud—she hadn't planned on nor anticipated relinquishing her control. "Believe it or not, I don't normally allow perfect strangers to bring me to orgasm."

His lips twitched. "I know I make a good first impression, but I'm hardly perfect." His hands skimmed down her back. "And I wouldn't say we're strangers, either."

"We are in all the ways that really count. We know next to nothing about each other."

"In that we don't know each other's favorite color, movie, book, or song, that's true. As for me making you forget everything…right back at ya. Losing control and forgetting restraint? Same goes for me. Believe it or not, I don't normally attempt to bring perfect strangers to orgasm."

Riley shifted, and his erection jerked against her stomach. "Things were very one-sided."

His grin turned lopsided. "I'm not complaining. But I can't deny I wish I'd thought to bring a condom. Listen, about this stranger thing…I think we should do something about that." He trailed a single fingertip down her wet arm, eliciting a barrage of goose bumps. "Will you have dinner with me tonight?"

"Dinner?" she repeated, her voice filled with skepticism.

"Yes. Dinner. You know, people sharing a meal. A glass of wine. Conversation. All for the sake of becoming better acquainted so they're not strangers anymore."

"I already have dinner plans for this evening."

"Oh." A muscle jerked in his jaw. "You said last night you weren't involved with anyone."

Riley slipped her arms from around him, then stepped back to put several feet between them. "I'm not," she said coolly. "If I were, this would not have happened. Actually, you also already have dinner plans for this evening. Remember Marcus? Our boss? Cookout?"

He dragged his hands down his face. "I'd totally forgotten. Seems that you're hell on my concentration. How about after dinner? Drinks at the Marriott?"

Riley's hormones and her common sense exchanged some stinging punches. She knew damn well that a hell of a lot more than drinks would happen if she joined him at the Marriott. If only he were any other guy... After a brief, bloody battle, common sense emerged as the victor and she shook her head.

"Jackson, I—"

He halted her words by placing his fingers against her lips. "Don't answer now. Think about it. We won't talk about work—won't even mention the W word." His finger slipped from her mouth and her tongue peeked out to touch the tingling spot. His eyes darkened, but he didn't touch her. Instead, he nodded toward the beach. "We'd better head back before they send out a search party for us."

Riley nodded her agreement and they waded back to the beach. After donning their life vests, they pushed the Jet Ski into the water. Riley climbed on behind Jackson and wrapped her arms around him. As they sped back to the house, she tried to corral her turbulent thoughts into some semblance of order, but her body and her mind were unfortunately pulling her in diametrically opposed directions. Her body unwisely told her to indulge in a one-night affair with Jackson. Her head wisely said stay away from him and concentrate on finding a different, more suitable man to jump back into the singles arena with.

WOULD SHE show up?

Jackson paced the length of his hotel room, pausing to tunnel his fingers through his hair. His gaze swiveled to the time glowing red from the digital clock for the umpteenth time. Nearly 10:00 p.m. This was the second night in a row that he'd experienced this gut-clenching uncertainty, wondering whether the woman who had his libido in a raging uproar would show up. The fact that Marcus Thornton's party had ended three hours ago didn't bode well for her accepting his invitation. Neither did the fact that she'd steered clear of him once they'd arrived back at the house after their Jet Ski ride. Before he'd departed for the Marriott, however, he'd pulled her aside and given her his room key and quietly asked her to use it. And for the last three hours, he'd tortured himself by alternately wondering whether she would come to him and asking himself why the hell he cared so much. What was it about her that had him so uncharacteristically unsettled? It wasn't as if he'd never experienced sparks before.

Yeah, but he'd never experienced anything like this. As if he'd been zapped with a Taser gun.

He dragged his hands down his face. Damn it, he needed to relax. Needed to think about something else. Needed to—

Answer the door.

The soft knock nearly stopped his heart. Was it Riley? If so, she'd obviously decided not to use the key he'd given her. He hoped it was her and not some hotel maintenance guy wanting to check the temperature controls, or someone delivering a fax. He took a few seconds to draw in a deep, careful breath. Then he strode to the door and pulled it opened.

Riley stood in the hallway, her dark, curly hair

loose around her shoulders, a flirtatious half smile curving her lips. She wore faded jeans that clung to her curves and a neon-yellow T-shirt decorated with an image of a chocolate chip cookie and the words The Sweetest Thing. Her cute pink-tipped toes peeked at him from sandals with blue, green, yellow, and orange crisscrossing straps. She carried a white square box tied with a red string that bore the same logo as her shirt.

"Need your fortune told?" she asked in a low, smoky voice that raised his temperature into the fever zone.

His stomach did that thing—what had she called it? Bloop? He gripped the doorknob to keep from reaching out and snatching her into his arms. "Sure—although I've gotta tell ya, it's looking very good. You didn't use your key."

"I thought it more polite to knock, in case you'd fallen asleep or something."

"Sleep is the *last* thing on my mind." Heat kindled in her gaze at his response, and he stepped back, waving his hand for her to enter. "Glad you could make it."

"You're going to be even gladder when you see what I've brought you." She stepped over the threshold, waggling the box under his nose and he caught a whiff of something sweet and delicious.

After he'd closed the door, he leaned back against the panel and said, "I didn't think you were going to come." He hadn't necessarily meant to say that, but the words plopped out of his mouth before he could stop them.

Riley set the box on the luggage rack just inside the door, then, with her heart pounding in anticipation, she turned to face him. Good God, the man was gorgeous. With several ebony strands spilling over his forehead, it looked as if he'd shoved impatient fingers through his dark hair. A white Polo shirt stretched across his broad chest, hinting at the impressive display of muscles she knew the soft cotton covered. Jeans, clearly comfortable old favorites based on the intriguing fade patterns, hugged his legs in a way that made her wish she had X ray vision. But no matter. She intended to have those pants off him soon enough.

Opting for the unpainted truth, she said, "I wasn't going to come. Believe me, I tried really hard to convince myself that I didn't want to be here with you. But it's been a while since I've allowed myself to indulge in something fun, and as we accountants are so fond of doing, I finally had to look at the bottom line. And the bottom line is that regardless of the fact that your name is Jackson Lange, I wanted to make love with you."

His eyes darkened with unmistakable desire. "As a marketing man, I'm normally not fond of the way accountants adhere to the bottom line, but in this case, I'm all for it."

"And then there's my sense of fair play," she said, her gaze wandering down to linger on his crotch before meeting his eyes once again. "I, um, owe you one."

"Can't wait to collect." He pushed off from the door, erasing the distance between them in a single stride. Riley backed up a step and her shoulders bumped into the wall. Bracketing her in by bracing his hands on the paneling on either side of her head, he leaned down and touched his tongue to the side of her neck.

A breathy laugh escaped her. "Don't you want to see what I brought you?"

"Delicious as it smelled, you smell better." He nibbled on her earlobe. "Hmm. And taste better."

"You might change your mind once you check out your treat."

"Very doubtful. This treat right here…" he ran the tip of his tongue over her sensitive lower lip, "is too delectable to be surpassed."

Riley ran hungry, eager hands up his chest to his shoulders. "You know, I came here with my control all intact," she said, rising up on her toes to nip tiny kisses across his jaw between words, "planning to slowly seduce and savor you, but, well, here I am thirty seconds in, and already you've messed up all my fine plans."

He grasped her hips and yanked her against him. Even through the layers of their jeans, his arousal was obvious, fueling the heat already coursing through her. "My control was shot to hell long before I even opened the door. As great as slow seduction and savoring sounds, I vote we save it for Round Two. Agreed?"

"God, yes."

In a heartbeat, they grabbed at each other like starved creatures presented with a feast. Their mouths melded in a frantic mating of lips and tongues, while their hands desperately sought to shed clothing. Breaking off their kiss, ragged breaths pumping from her lungs, she yanked his shirt from his jeans and tugged it impatiently upward. He grasped the ends, pulled the material over his head, and sent the garment flying across the room while Riley quickly stripped off her own shirt.

"Nice bra," he said, eyeing the ridiculously expensive bit of lace covering her breasts while he toed off his sneakers and jerked off his socks.

"Thanks." She unhooked the black lacy garment and dropped it to the floor, a tactical error, she realized as he instantly cupped her breasts in his hands and lowered his head to lave her nipples, distracting him from removing his jeans. She pressed her shoulders against the wall, arrows of want shooting through her with each delicious pull of his lips on her nipples, and simultaneously kicked off her sandals and applied shaking fingers to her jeans. After sliding down her zipper, she reached in her back pocket for the condom she'd put there.

"Condom," she gasped.

He ran his tongue up her chest and feasted on her neck while his hands continued to torment her breasts. "Have some. In nightstand."

"Have one. Right here." She slapped the plastic packet against his chest with one hand and shimmied down her jeans and panties with the other. She spent all of two seconds lamenting that he wouldn't see the black wisp of lace thong that matched her bra, but these were desperate times. Urgent desire scorched through her veins like molten lava, stripping away everything except the frantic need to be naked and have him inside her *now*.

While she worked to kick her jeans aside, he unfastened his Levi's and shoved them and his boxer briefs down far enough to free his erection, then he quickly rolled on the condom. Reaching behind her, he grasped her buttocks and lifted her. Riley gripped his shoulders, clasped her legs around his hips, then breathed out a long moan as he entered her with a single heart-stopping thrust.

His rough, ragged breaths mingled with hers as he stroked her, hard, fast, relentless. There was no gentle warning to the onset of the fierce orgasm that dragged a harsh cry of pleasure from her throat. Her fingers clenched his shoulders, and her legs tightened around his hips as spasms of fiery pleasure convulsed through her. With a feral groan, he thrust upward one final time, then lowered his forehead to the spot where her neck and shoulder met and joined her with his own release.

Their panting breaths intermingled, and after a few seconds, a puff of laughter escaped Riley. "We sound like we just ran a marathon."

"Didn't we?"

"Maybe. Who won?"

"Not sure. Why don't we just call it a tie?"

"Sounds good." She managed to lift her head and a feminine thrill zoomed through her at his glazed expression. "So, I guess my debt of honor is paid."

"Can't argue with that. Nice going, having a condom in your back pocket."

"I wasn't sure if you'd be dressed for the party, and I wanted to be prepared—although it hadn't occurred to me that we'd need it quite so quickly. Or quite so close to the door."

Keeping her wedged between his body and the wall, he leaned forward to nuzzle her neck with his warm lips, while his hands gently kneaded her butt. "Didn't mean to fall on you the minute you walked in, but you have this very destructive effect on my self-control."

"Did you hear me complaining? Besides, it's clear you have the same effect on me." A fact she found decidedly unsettling, but one she'd examine later.

"That the only condom you have?"

"Two more."

"Good. With the dozen I bought on my way back to the hotel, that ought to last us the night."

His husky words rasped warmly across her ear, eliciting a breathless laugh. "That's a lot of condoms for one night."

"Maybe we'll set a new world's record."

"Maybe we'll end up in the emergency room."

"Are there any hospitals near here?"

"Several."

"Then we're covered."

He gently eased himself from her, and her legs slid down from his hips. When her feet touched the floor, she had to lock her knees to steady herself. While she pushed her tangled hair from her face, Jackson stripped off his jeans and underwear the rest of the way, then murmured, "Be right back," before stepping into the bathroom, presumably to dispose of the condom. Her admiring gaze zeroed in on his extremely fine rear before he disappeared from her sight. Whew. The back view was as scrumptious as the front view.

Pulling in a few much-needed deep breaths, she eyed his pile of discarded clothes. Boxer briefs, she noted. She bet he'd look great wearing nothing but that soft cotton. God knows he looked really great *not* wearing that soft cotton.

He emerged from the bathroom and moved to stand directly in front of her. Reaching for her hands, he entwined their fingers and his gaze roamed slowly over her, a favor she returned.

"No doubt about it, there's some very nice DNA swimming around in your gene pool, Jackson."

He smiled. "Funny, I was just thinking that you'd hit some sort of genetic jackpot."

She basked in the warm glow of feminine satisfaction brought on by his compliment and avid, admiring gaze. "Thank you. Thanks to you, I can barely feel my knees. Now I know what overcooked spaghetti feels like."

He waggled his brows. "I know just the thing to make you feel better."

She laughed, reveling in a delicious sense of freedom, and waggled right back at him. "I bet."

"I do. Really. Guess what I've got?"

"An incredible body?"

"Thank you. But not the answer I'm looking for."

"A sexy smile?"

"Again, I thank you, but not the correct answer."

"Magical hands? Gorgeous lips? Great ass?"

"Back at ya, sweetheart, but still not right."

"Very good odds of getting lucky again really soon?"

A sexy half grin pulled up one corner of his mouth. "Good to know."

"Is it the right answer?"

"'Fraid not."

"Then I give up. I've never done well at guessing games."

"So I see. But that's okay. Believe me, you're plenty good at other stuff. I've got a fabulous whirlpool tub right in the bathroom. I was thinking you, me, and a soothing soak, along with whatever you brought in that bakery box would be a nice way to recover before Round Two begins." He released her hands, then lightly kneaded her breasts, pebbling her nipples into aroused peaks.

A low purr vibrated in her throat. "The contents of that box will require something to drink."

"Wine?"

"Nope. Got milk?"

"Nope. But I've got room service."

"Right. Then let's say two cappuccinos. I have the

feeling we'll need the caffeine before the night is over." She then tried to adopt her most businesslike tone, but it was damned difficult with his magic fingers tormenting her breasts. "And if you think I'll okay an expense of cappuccinos...ooh, that feels good...ordered from room service for the express use of seducing a female guest, you're sadly mistaken."

"Dragon lady," he said with a lazy smile.

"Spendthrift," she returned with an answering grin.

"You know, Madame Sees-All told me that my lady in the red dress wanted to make all my sensual dreams come true. And then she wanted me to return the favor." His gaze roamed slowly over her body, heating her skin. "It's time for me to return the favor."

5

"I WOULD BE hard-pressed to name anything better than this." Riley sat in the whirlpool tub and blew a long sigh of contented pleasure. "I feel like a pampered goddess."

"Glad to hear it," came the husky rumble of Jackson's deep voice near her ear.

"Warm, relaxing water swirling all around, a frothy cappuccino, being fed bite-sized tidbits of Boston Cream doughnuts, a fabulous pillow…" She wriggled slightly, brushing her back against the muscular wall of Jackson's chest, luxuriating in the feel of him surrounding her as she lounged in front of him, his arms and legs bracketing hers, her head resting on his shoulder, the hard length of his erection nestled snugly against her buttocks, promising that Round Two loomed on the not-too-distant horizon. "Mmm. And the company's not bad, either."

"Back at ya. Want another piece of doughnut?"

"Do dogs say *woof*?"

He chuckled, then held a particularly tempting morsel, complete with a glistening smear of chocolate and a dollop of cream about six inches from her mouth.

Grasping his wrist, she pulled his hand to her lips and ate the offering. After swallowing, she ran her tongue over his fingers, sucking each one into her mouth to capture every last crumb and bit of chocolate glaze. He groaned and shifted, pressing his erection more firmly against her buttocks. "Delicious," she said when she'd finished.

"For me, too, and I didn't even eat any. Want another piece?"

She chuckled at the exaggerated hopeful note in his voice. "I'm good for now, thanks." She settled her head more comfortably against his shoulder and let her eyes drift closed. He slipped his hands under the water and rested them on her midriff, moving his thumbs slowly back and forth so that they just brushed the undersides of her breasts.

"How is it that you aren't involved with anyone?" he asked, his warm breath tickling past her ear as he nuzzled her neck. "Did you recently break up with someone? Nursing a broken heart?"

She shook her head. "Most recent parting of the ways was a couple of months ago, but there was no broken heart involved. He was just the latest in a string of infrequent, incompatible dates who illustrated once again that while the immediate attraction is to the handsome guy, good looks do not always equal good character. Turned out we had almost nothing in common, proving beyond any doubt that while opposites might attract at first, they don't make it for long."

She stretched her neck to give his marauding lips better access. "But most of the blame sits squarely on my shoulders. Between the hours I put in at work and my high-maintenance sister, I don't have much time or energy left for dating. And since I don't have much time for it, I tend to be very impatient with all the games and crap that go along with it. I'm a 'cut to the chase, show me the bottom line, don't feed me a load of bull' sort of gal. I've found that a lot of men are threatened or put off by that. Nor are they very understanding of my situation with Tara."

"Tara's your sister?"

"Yes. And my roommate for the last five years."

"Younger than you?"

"Yes. Just graduated from college—finally. She's starting a job in a few weeks and is preparing to move out."

"How do you feel about that?"

"Honestly? I'm relieved. I love her, but she isn't an easy person to live with. Of course, she'd say the exact same thing about me."

"Why was she living with you instead of on campus?"

She turned to look at him and made a face. "You really want to hear all this?"

"I do."

"Why?"

His thumbs continued their hypnotic stroking. "I'm curious about you. And sympathetic. My younger brother lived with me for a year and it was *not* an easy year. We can exchange 'love 'em, but they're a pain in the ass' sibling war stories."

A huff of laughter escaped Riley. "Sounds like you've met Tara."

"Only because she sounds just like my brother Brian."

Riley nodded. "Tara is very intelligent, but during her senior year in high school she totally lost focus. Our mom died after a yearlong illness and Dad just...lost it. He couldn't cope and basically checked out on us emotionally. I was already living on my own and better able to deal with Dad's emotional distance than Tara, although it was still really difficult. Tara, who'd always been a party girl, just completely went off the deep end. She went away to college and ended up failing every class, except Intro to Yoga. She eked out a D in that. And she was involved with a guy, who for lack of a better term, was a complete dirt bag. My dad had moved to Florida—he couldn't stand living in the house without Mom. After much begging on my part, he finally joined a grief counseling group, but even after he started inching his way back from his grief, he was totally incapable of dealing with Tara."

"So you stepped in and offered to take over."

"That's the bottom line, yes. Tara claimed she wanted to go back to college, but Dad refused to pay more tuition to subsidize a party lifestyle. She promised she'd do better but he said he wouldn't pay for her to live on campus. So I offered that she could stay with me. The deal was struck that as long as she lived with me and made passing grades, he'd pay for her education."

"A generous offer you made."

Riley shrugged. "She's my sister. She needed help. Although, when I made the offer, I was thinking more of my dad. I didn't want him to have any more on his plate. As for Tara, I knew she was still grieving. I was, too. But she seemed to think that our mom's death was a valid excuse for her to get away with anything and everything. I grew pretty disgusted with her. I know we all do stupid stuff when we're eighteen, but it really pushed my buttons that she was handed a golden opportunity for a college education and she was hell-bent on frittering it away."

She blew out a long sigh. "Tara isn't a bad person, but she's irresponsible. Careless. With people, their feelings, her possessions. Other people's possessions. Keeping her in line, trying to provide a stable home and good example, being there for her during the almost daily dramatic crises that litter her life, has required a lot of energy, patience and time over the past five years."

"Sounds like you deserve a medal."

Riley frowned and shook her head. "No. I didn't mean for it to sound that way. I *wanted* to do it. It was my choice, and I don't have any regrets. In the past five years, Tara has grown up a lot, and even though we argue—a lot—and she still has a great deal of maturing to do, I'm really proud of her. She took classes every summer and winter break to make up the year she flunked out. And while she barely squeaked by in a number of classes, she managed to graduate. The job she accepted is in South Carolina, so she'll only be a few hours' drive away from me in one direction, and our dad in the other."

"And how's your dad doing now?"

"He's great." A smile pulled at her lips. "He recently started seeing someone—a widow who lives in his complex. I called him a few days ago and he sounded really happy. It was good to hear."

She reached for her coffee mug, and after taking a soothing sip, she said, "And that's more than you ever wanted to know about me. Your turn. What brought about your living arrangement with your brother?"

"Brian spent his first two years of school at a community college and lived at home. Then he was accepted to NYU, but the tuition alone was killer, let alone the cost of living on campus. I already lived in Manhattan, so, thinking I'd ease the financial burden, I said Brian could live with me while he went to school. But I'm nine years older than Brian, so I hadn't actually lived with him for a long time. Little did I know what I was letting myself in for."

Riley reached back and patted his cheek with her wet hand. "Been there, done that, bleeding for you. How long ago was this?"

"Two years ago. For his senior year at NYU, he scored a part-time job and shared an apartment with five other guys. I visited their digs once, and if you think you have any inkling of the mess six college guys can make, you're wrong."

"Are you close with Brian?"

"Yeah, but we're night-and-day different. I'm not saying Brian isn't a good person—he'd give you the shirt off his back, although you might want to have it laundered before you wore it. He graduated NYU last year, landed a good job and lives in a nice apartment with a revolving set of roommates, but he still hasn't matured out of that 'frat boy' stage. His idea of a perfect weekend is attending a rowdy sports event with the guys and hooking up with a woman who has a centerfold figure, wears hoochie-mama clothes, and who, after sex, will serve him an ice-cold beer."

Riley couldn't help but giggle. "I thought that was every man's idea of the perfect weekend."

"Not exactly." He dipped his chin and caught her earlobe gently between his teeth, shooting a battalion of tingles down her spine.

"So then what *is* your idea of a perfect weekend?"

"Well, *this* weekend has turned out pretty good."

"*Pretty* good?"

"Stupendously good."

"Even though I don't wear hoochie-mama clothes?"

"Honey, you don't need to wear hoochie-mama

clothes. And what's under the clothes you do wear...have mercy." He lightly scraped his teeth down the side of her neck.

"So...why is a guy like you unattached?"

"A guy like me?"

"Employed. Heterosexual. Has his own living quarters." She ran her fingers over his muscular thigh. "Reasonably attractive."

He chuckled at her backhanded compliment, then said, "I was engaged, but that ended ten months ago. I've dated, but like you, I get tired of the hassles and the games and the demands."

"Amen to that."

"So, I guess I'm unattached because I haven't met anyone I wanted to be attached to."

"What happened with your fiancée—or would you rather not talk about it?"

She felt his shoulders move in a shrug. "Not much to tell. We'd been engaged about two months when she flew to Chicago to attend a college reunion where she was reunited with an old boyfriend. Apparently he was 'the one who got away' and she decided she didn't want to let him get away a second time."

She turned her head and pressed a kiss against the base of his throat. "I'm sorry. I know how that betrayal hurts."

"Right. The picnic table guy you mentioned."

"And he wasn't even my fiancé." She resettled her head on his shoulder and lightly ran her fingers along his thighs. "Are you still in love with her?"

"No. I can't deny it hurt like hell at the time, but I've moved on." A laugh rumbled in his throat, vibrating against her temple. "Now I have to protect myself against the matchmaking efforts of my mother and sister, who, based on the amount of time they spend trying to arrange my love life, clearly have too much time on their hands."

His voice tapered off, until the only sound was the quiet whirr of the jets. Riley snuggled back a bit, and Jackson's hands moved lower on her stomach, his long fingers easing along the crease of her thighs. A purr vibrated in Riley's throat and she reached up and back to loop her arms lightly around his neck, her wet fingers dampening the hair at his nape.

"Hungry yet?" he asked, gently worrying her earlobe between his teeth.

"Yeah. But not for doughnuts." Her words ended on a breathy gasp as his fingers dipped lower to lazily circle her feminine flesh. "And that's not a sentence that normally passes my lips."

"No doughnuts? Then what do you want?"

"You're off to a good start…maybe a little…ooh, yeah, right there."

She spread her legs wider. "How do you feel about sex in the bathtub?"

"Torture. Really. I'd hate it a lot." He blew out an exaggerated, put-upon sigh. "But if it's what you want, I'll take it on the chin and try to bear it."

"That's what I like—a team player."

"That's me. Always willing to go that extra mile. Hang on to me."

Riley tightened her grip around the back of his neck and he hooked his hands under her knees, lifting her legs up and over his spread legs, leaving her thighs widely splayed. One of his large, wet hands teased her nipples, while the other slipped between her legs and stroked with unerring perfection.

Watching his hands roam over her, Riley arched her back and pushed her hips upward to meet his questing fingers. The sight of his fingers gliding over, teasing her nipples, his other hand curved over her mound while his unseen fingers caressed her, then slipped inside her, aroused her beyond bearing. He deepened his strokes and a long moan of pleasure escaped her. Turning her head, she nipped at his neck. "I want you inside me when I come."

"Right where I want to be." He slowly released her and, breathing hard, she turned around, kneeled, then reached for the condom he'd set on the side of the tub. He lifted his hips, and she quickly sheathed him. Then she straddled him, gripped his shoulders and slowly sank down on his erection, luxuriating in the sensation of him filling her while the heated water curled around them. He leaned forward and suckled her breasts as his hands cruised down her back to curve around her buttocks, letting her set the rhythm.

Determined not to relinquish her control so quickly this time, she kept to a leisurely pace, threw her head back, closed her eyes and lost herself in the sensations infusing her. But it wasn't long before his upward thrusts gained momentum and her control evaporated. Their pace increased, and at the first stirrings of her release, a long *ooh* of pleasure escaped her.

"Now," she whispered.

Her orgasm overtook her, rapid-fire pulses of pleasure throbbing through her system. His hold tightened on her hips and, with a low groan, he buried his face between her breasts. She wrapped her arms around his head and held him tightly against her pounding heart, shuddering with the delightful aftershocks rumbling through her.

When her breathing returned to something resembling normal, she unwound her arms from around him. He tipped up his chin and shot her a wicked half grin.

"Whew. Gotta tell ya, Riley, you really shoot that whole 'dull, boring accountant' stereotype right out of the bathtub water."

"I'm dull and boring at work."

"Must be the material, not the woman, 'cause dull and boring you are not."

A secret inner smile pulled at her. Clearly she was well on her way to recapturing her former self. "Thanks." She ran her fingertip down his nose and smiled. "*Now* I'm ready for that doughnut."

LATE MONDAY MORNING, after a productive breakfast meeting with Marcus Thornton and Paul Stanfield where future projects were discussed, Jackson rode up the elevator with the CEO and CFO to Prestige's offices so Jackson could meet members of the Atlanta staff. He couldn't deny that there was one particular staff member he was anxious to see again. He just hoped that when he saw Riley the first thing that plopped out of his mouth wasn't, "Let's get naked and pick up where we left off last night."

"Great group we have working here," Marcus said. "Top-notch team."

Jackson gave himself a mental shake and forced his attention away from thoughts of last night. He didn't doubt that Marcus, who'd been in the commercial building business for over thirty years and was very well respected, would have anything less than a great support unit behind him. Jackson was proud to be part of that team. He hoped his efforts to bring Prestige and Elite together would result in a merger that would propel his career further up the corporate ladder.

They exited the elevators, then did the rounds. Jackson met some new folks and renewed his acquaintance with several others who had attended Marcus's cookout at the lake yesterday. Every time they moved toward a new office or group of cubicles, his heart sped up in anticipation, wondering if he was about to come face-to-face with Riley.

Riley. Good God, the woman hadn't been out of his thoughts for a nanosecond. Images of them making love filled every corner of his mind, making it difficult to concentrate on the small talk he'd been forced to make this morning. Following Marcus and Paul, they rounded the final corner, and instantly he saw the shiny brass plate that read Riley Addison on the last office door. The door was open, and Marcus knocked lightly as the three of them filed in. "Morning, Riley."

She swiveled her chair around from where she'd been frowning at her computer screen and looked up at her visitors.

And bloop went his stomach.

She gracefully stood and smiled. "Good morning, Marcus. Paul. Jackson."

Nothing in her expression or her voice gave any indication that only a few hours ago they'd been naked together—a fact that shouldn't have bothered him, but on some level did. Probably because he suddenly felt as if he were running a fever, while she looked perfectly calm and cool.

"Just bringing Jackson around to see the offices and meet some more of the staff before he leaves for the airport," Paul said.

"What do you think of our place here, Jackson?" she asked.

"Nice setup. Very open and interactive." He smiled into her eyes. "Very nice people."

Marcus looked at his watch then said, "Paul and I have a conference call scheduled in five minutes, so we need to go. Riley, would you mind taking over and seeing Jackson back to the elevators?"

"No problem," she said.

After shaking hands with Marcus and Paul, Jackson found himself alone with Riley in her office. Staring at her. Heart pounding. And very uncharacteristically tongue-tied. She wore a cream-colored pleated skirt with a sleeveless sweater in graduating shades of orange and yellow that reminded him of a tropical sunset. Her chestnut curls were held back with some sort of doodad that, while making for a very attractive style, he still itched to remove from her hair so he could sift his fingers through the silky strands. As he'd done last night. While he'd been buried deep inside her body. The thought arrowed heat straight through him.

She came around her desk and leaned her hips against the dark wood, her hands curling over the edge. Her skirt hit just above her knees, and she wore pale yellow high-heeled pumps that did incredible things to her already incredible legs. How was it that every guy in Atlanta wasn't lined up outside her office door?

He cleared his throat and nodded toward the mountain of paperwork on her desk. "Looks like you're snowed under."

"A bit. I've been working like a dog on a presentation for a meeting with Paul tomorrow afternoon." A half smile curved her lips. "I think I'm suffering from a severe case of PowerPoint poisoning."

He laughed. "I have about fifteen minutes before

I need to leave for the airport and I'm desperate for coffee. I thought I'd grab some in the café downstairs. May I buy you a cup?"

"If you'll spring for a colossal latte with an extra shot of espresso, you're on. I definitely need the caffeine. I, uh, didn't get much sleep last night."

"In that case, we'll make it two colossals with an extra shot."

A look filled with sensual awareness and knowledge bounced between them, and he barely resisted the urge to jerk at his suddenly constrictive necktie. Then she pushed off from the desk and walked past him into the hallway, leaving the subtle scent of vanilla in her wake. He followed her, trying with little success to keep his wandering gaze on the back of her head rather than her shapely butt—which he now knew bore a tiny trio of beguiling freckles on her left cheek. After they walked by the receptionist's desk, they passed through heavy glass doors bearing the Prestige logo to the bank of elevators. Riley reached out and pushed the Down arrow.

Looking at her profile, he said the words that had echoed through his mind all morning. "Last night was…incredible."

She turned her head and he noted the flare of heat in her caramel eyes. "To coin one of your phrases, back at ya."

"You were gone when I woke up." It had surprised him how much that had bothered him, how cold and lonely the bed had seemed without her. How much he'd wanted her to be the first thing he'd seen when he'd awoken. How disappointed he'd been to find she'd left.

"I needed to go home to catch a couple hours of

sleep and then get ready for work. I thought you might wake up when I kissed you goodbye, but you were dead to the world."

"Because someone wore me out, but good."

"Is that a complaint?" she asked with a teasing glint in her eyes. "Because we can stop at the complaint department. It's on the third floor."

He stepped closer to her, liking the way her pupils dilated. "Oh, yeah. I absolutely hate it when a gorgeous, sexy woman makes love with me until I can't move a muscle. Really."

The elevator doors slid open, and they stepped into the empty car. The instant the doors closed behind them, Jackson gave in to the desire clawing at him and backed her against the wall. "Good morning," he said, then kissed her deeply, his tongue seeking to sample again all the delicious heat he'd tasted last night. She moaned and returned his kiss, her arms slipping around his waist, her hands sliding down to his buttocks to pull him tighter against her. His body reacted swiftly, blood rushing to his groin, and with a groan, he skimmed his hands over the feminine curves he'd explored last night.

A faint *ding* penetrated the fog of lust engulfing him. With a gasp, she broke off their kiss then stepped swiftly away from him, smoothing hands he noted weren't quite steady over her sweater and skirt. He winced and adjusted himself as best he could, thankful he wore a double breasted suit as the jacket camouflaged his aroused state. The doors *whooshed* open and a cool blast of air-conditioning hit him, a welcome relief since it felt like his skin was on fire.

They headed across the dark green marble-tile

lobby, her heels tapping against the shiny floor, and he shoved his fists in his pockets to keep from reaching for her hand.

"I'm not sure I need that colossal latte anymore," she said in a husky undertone, throwing him a sideways glance. "That kiss was a pretty potent jolt to the system."

"You can say that again." A jolt he sure as hell hadn't wanted to end so abruptly.

They entered the café, and after Jackson ordered their lattes, Riley smiled at the cashier and said, "And two Boston Creams, Michael."

Michael shot her a broad grin. "You got it, Riley."

"They get their doughnuts from The Sweetest Thing," Riley said to Jackson. "Thought you might like one for the road."

An image flooded his mind of them lounging in the whirlpool tub, naked, sated, laughing, sipping cappuccinos and feeding each other the fabulous doughnuts.

"I'd never say no to Boston Cream."

Jackson carried their tray to a table in the far corner. Once they were seated, he held up his foam cup. "To…" he hesitated, realizing that what he wanted to say—to more incredible nights together—was probably inappropriate.

"To good health and success," she supplied, tapping her white plastic lid against his.

Jackson took a sip of the hot brew, savoring the caffeine easing through his system, then topped it off with bite of doughnut. "I always thought the Boston Creams at my local bakery were the best, but these," he waved the doughnut in front of his nose and breathed in the sweet smell, "are just as good."

She bit into her doughnut, closed her eyes and

chewed with a rapturous expression that stilled him, halting his hand halfway to his mouth. She ate with the same passion she'd displayed last night, a fact that did nothing to relieve the ache in his groin.

"I like that you're clearly not a slave to some low-carb diet," he said, watching her. Wanting her. "I don't think I've ever seen anyone eat with such enjoyment."

After she swallowed, her eyelids fluttered opened and their eyes met. "I love food," she said. For the space of several heartbeats, they simply looked at each other, palpable awareness filling the space between them. Then she averted her gaze and broke off a tiny piece of doughnut.

"I don't even want to think about how many extra miles I'm going to have to put in on the treadmill to work off all the doughnuts I've eaten in the last eight hours," she said, then popped the morsel into her mouth.

Jackson took a slow sip of his coffee and tried to beat back his desire. Finally, he curved his lips into a smirk and said, "That's your fourth."

She cocked a brow. "What are you, keeping score?"

"Absolutely. I'm surprised you're not, what with you being a numbers gal and all."

"Oh, I knew I'd had four. I was just trying to forget."

"Well, I think plenty of calories were burned off last night." He rested his forearms on the round mosaic tile table and leaned toward her. "Especially during Round Three."

A delicate blush suffused her cheeks, surprising and charming him. It required a great deal of will power not to reach out and brush his fingers over that alluring wash of color.

"Hmm, Round Three," she repeated softly. "Yes, that was quite athletic."

"You're delightfully…flexible."

"Glad to know my yoga class is paying off."

He leaned back and studied her. She took several sips of her coffee, then asked, "What? Do I have Boston Cream on my face?"

"No. I was just…wondering about you. We sort of did things backward. Usually people date a few times—hell, at least *once*—before sleeping together. I find that I'm curious about you. About your life. Your likes and dislikes. I'd like to…know you."

"Believe me, after last night, you know things about me that even my best friend doesn't know."

He smiled. "I meant in other than the biblical sense. I guess what I'm trying to say is that you turned out to be nothing like I expected, and you… and last night…were very pleasant surprises."

"You mean for a fire-breathing dragon lady?"

"Exactly. Although I admit it wasn't an apt description."

"Actually, it's a very apt description, at least when it comes to business—and something you'll recall once you get back to work. Which is where we are now— back to work. Back to reality. Back to marketing versus accounting. Back to clashing department heads."

She was right, of course. So why did a frisson of annoyance seep through him? "Wait till the dragon lady sees my expense report for this weekend. She's gonna bust a gut."

"Don't think I won't go over it with a fine-tooth comb and demand proper documentation." She leaned forward. "And don't even try to put through those cappuccinos."

"Not even as an entertainment expense?"

"No way. That definitely wasn't for schmoozing a client."

"I guess you're right. It just wouldn't be seemly to document on my expense report that the cappuccino was for a hot hoochie mama who had her wicked way with me. Three times."

"Exactly. It specifically states in the company handbook that no reimbursement will be made for the entertaining of hot hoochie mamas."

"Good to know. So, what does Madame Sees-All predict for our future?" He tossed out the question lightly, but for reasons he didn't care to examine his every nerve ending felt on red alert, waiting for her answer.

She pursed her lips, drawing his attention to their ripe fullness, filling his mind with the memory of the feel of them, their sweet taste. "She predicts some initial 'I've-seen-you-naked' awkwardness, but it will fade quickly as things return to normal."

"Normal?"

"Abrupt marketing demands, equally abrupt accounting denials. Terse e-mails. Aggravation. Improperly documented expense reports." She smiled. "You know, normal."

"Maybe now relations between our departments will improve. After all, we got along well together outside of work."

"Yes, but only because we'd agreed not to discuss work. Now we're back at the office. And you're on your way home to New York, where you live—nine hundred miles from here. All we have is work."

She was right. Wasn't she? Yes, of course she was.

He was only having difficulty accepting it because she was so close…so tantalizingly close. As soon as he got the hell out of Dodge, his head would get straight again. Still, he could easily imagine spending another night with Riley in his bed.

"Does Madame Sees-All divine anything else?"

"Like what?"

"Like maybe you coming to New York for a weekend?" He watched her carefully, telling himself that it was the caffeine making his heart pound so hard. He tried to discern her thoughts, but her expression was impossible to read.

Finally she said, "That's very tempting, but—"

"I've found that nothing good generally comes after the word but. Listen, I know from experience that any attraction this hot will burn itself out quickly. But it somehow doesn't feel quite burned out yet."

"Maybe not, but I know from experience that while opposites can initially attract, that attraction fizzles fast."

"I agree. So it's not like we're in this for the long haul. More like a quick jaunt around the park."

"You're suggesting we set aside all the reasons this is a bad idea and go out with a blaze of glory."

"I am."

"As tempting as your invitation is, as tempting as you are, it's just not a good idea."

"Why?"

"You even need to ask? Our work situation is already complicated enough without adding sex to the mix."

"Too late. We've already added sex to the mix."

"Okay, then without adding *more* sex. You were

here, we were attracted, we acted upon it. End of story. Making anything more out of it would be a mistake."

"I'm perfectly capable of keeping my professional and personal lives separate, Riley."

"Good for you. I'm not certain I am. Then there's the fact that, except for between the sheets, we barely know each other. Most of the little I do know—at least as it pertains to work—annoys me. On top of all that, we have zero in common, and since you live in New York, you're geographically undesirable. I see no point in prolonging something that is doomed to failure from the starting gate."

There was no pushing away the irritation pricking him. "Since we 'barely know each other'—a statement I don't agree with, by the way—how do you know we have zero in common?"

"The barrage of less-than-friendly e-mails we've exchanged gives me a pretty good idea. Since we're so different regarding our work ethics, it only makes sense that everything else would follow."

"Actually, I don't think our work ethics are all that different. We're both career-oriented and take our jobs seriously. As for non-work stuff, we both like doughnuts."

"*Everybody* likes doughnuts, Jackson."

"What about the fact that we've both suffered through living with our college-age siblings?"

"That's *one* thing. And most likely the *only* thing."

"You don't know that."

"No? I'll prove it. What's your favorite food?"

"Thai."

"Italian. Favorite type of movie?"

"Spy thriller."

"Romantic comedy. Favorite color?"

"Blue."

"Yellow. Favorite sport?"

"Tennis."

"Baseball. How'd you spend your last day off?"

"In bed. With you."

She blinked. "Before that."

He thought for a second, then said, "Shopped for my sister's birthday present, then took in the new exhibit at the Metropolitan Museum of Art."

"I give my sister gift certificates because she'd hate anything I picked out for her, and I haven't visited an art museum since my tenth grade class trip." She spread her hands. "See what I mean? Nothing in common."

"If the merger between Prestige and Elite goes through, the offices will most likely consolidate, probably here in Atlanta. Which means my job would move here."

Her brows hiked up. "You'd move to Atlanta?"

He hesitated, wondering what had possessed him to say that when relocating had never been on his radar screen. Finally, he said, "I honestly don't know. My plan has always been to climb the corporate ladder and make my mark in New York, but I suppose I'd consider a move if Prestige made me an offer I couldn't refuse."

"That's a lot of big ifs. And even *if* the merger happens, and *if* you moved here, then you'd only no longer be geographically undesirable. Instead, we'd just have nothing in common at a closer distance. And if you remain in New York, well, I just don't have the time, energy, or desire to get involved in a long-distance relationship."

"I can't disagree with any of your points. But then there's this…" He grasped her hand and brought it to his mouth, pressing a heated kiss against the pale skin of her inner wrist, a spot he'd discovered last night was highly sensitive.

Her eyes turned smoky and she pulled in a decidedly shaky breath as she gently extricated her hand. "Yes, there is that. But we've done that. So let's just leave it at...that."

He studied her for several seconds, but when he saw she was clearly resolved, he nodded. "All right."

Well, that was fine. Sure, he would've enjoyed another night with her, but she was right—they had little in common personally and even less in common professionally. Their sizzle would have fizzled out anyway, sooner rather than later.

He glanced at his watch, confused by the deep stab of regret hitting him that he needed to leave. "I have to go or I'll miss my flight. Thanks for an...enjoyable weekend."

"Ditto." She winked at him, and he cursed the fact that he was such a sucker for a wink. "Fix up that budget and I'll take a look at it."

He nodded and rose. "It's my top priority, along with submitting my latest expense report."

She rose as well. "Don't forget to attach your receipts. Have a safe trip back."

"Thanks." Damn it, he wanted to kiss her goodbye, but since he didn't want to place her in a possibly awkward situation if someone saw them he instead offered his hand. She placed her hand in his, and he experienced that same tingling whoosh he'd felt the instant he'd set eyes on her. "Goodbye, Riley."

"Bye, Jackson."

Forcing himself to release her, he then walked across the lobby, turning the corner to head toward the parking lot where he'd left his rental car. As soon as he was out of her sight, he pulled in a relieved breath. Okay. He'd had a great weekend. Some incredible sex. Some fabulous doughnuts. Some incredible sex. Sure, she was uppermost in his mind—right now. But once he got home and settled in back at work, Riley and this weekend would fade into a pleasant memory.

Yup, they sure would.

6

THE FOLLOWING Friday evening, Riley sat at her desk, painstakingly reviewing the second-quarter financial statements. Her phone rang, but she ignored it and let it go through to voice mail as the office had closed hours ago. Probably a wrong number anyway, and if not, she'd deal with whoever it was on Monday.

After completing the profit-and-loss and cash flow statements, her eyes needed a serious break from all those numbers. She leaned back in her chair and snagged the pickle from the foam take-out tray containing her turkey sandwich dinner. Munching on the pickle, she rolled her neck in an effort to relieve the tension tightening her shoulders. Her gaze flicked to the time posted in the corner of her computer screen and she groaned. Already eight-thirty. And she had at least another hour's worth of review and analysis ahead of her, not to mention the workload she planned to bring home to do over the weekend.

Needing a few more minutes away from the numbers dancing before her eyes, she bit into her sandwich and clicked on her e-mail. Her chewing halted when she saw that Jackson had sent her three e-mails—one just after three o'clock this afternoon, and the two others only about ten minutes ago. Obviously he was working late, as well. Her heart jumped in the same ridiculous way it had earlier in the week when he'd e-mailed his expense report for his trip to Atlanta.

Crazy, that's what it was. He'd left four days ago, yet it seemed he still occupied every inch of her mind. He intruded on her thoughts far too often, usually at very inconvenient times—like during a meeting yesterday with Marcus. One second she'd been listening intently to him, and the next she'd drifted off into a daydream, imagining Jackson, naked and aroused, looming over her, his eyes dark with need. She'd completely lost track of the conversation and the fire burning in her cheeks had obviously not gone unnoticed by Marcus as it prompted him to ask with his fatherly concern if she was feeling all right.

She'd opened the few e-mails Jackson had sent her this week with an eagerness that appalled her. She was further appalled by her acute disappointment that those e-mails had consisted of nothing more than cover letters for attached expense reports and receipts—all very properly documented—or his usual short, terse, correspondence. Her disappointment annoyed and confused her. What did she expect? That he'd make personal comments? Send flirty messages over the company e-mail? Of course not. So why did she feel so let down?

Swallowing her bite of sandwich, she clicked on the first message he'd sent earlier today. It was short and to the point, informing her he planned to send his revised marketing budget later today and requested it be given top priority.

The second e-mail was an update that had been sent to the company-wide distribution list regarding upcoming changes to Prestige's Web site. After reading the memo, she clicked on the third e-mail, which contained an attachment labeled Revised Marketing Budget. She quickly scanned the message which he'd sent with the attachment at 8:12 p.m.:

Took longer than anticipated to finish this, but am sending it now so you'll have it first thing Monday morning. I realize you're swamped and it's a lot to ask, but any priority you could give this would be greatly appreciated. Everything is in place to move forward, but my hands are tied without the additional funds. I also just left you a voice mail message regarding same to cover all my bases, just in case cyberspace somehow swallows my e-mail. Looking forward to hearing from you.

When she finished reading, she snatched up her phone and accessed her voice mail which advised her she had one new message, received at 8:16 p.m. this evening. With her heart pounding in the most absurd fashion, she gripped the receiver tightly and listened. Jackson's smooth, deep voice filtered into her ear, saying almost word for word what he'd stated in his e-mail. Her eyes drifted closed, and a vivid image of him materialized behind her eyelids. Tall, handsome, a teasing smile tilting the corners of his lovely mouth, his blue eyes gleaming with mischief and desire. When the message ended she replaced the receiver and worried her bottom lip, debating the wisdom of what she was considering.

"What the hell," she muttered, and snatched up the receiver. What did she have to lose except a few more hours of sleep? Besides, didn't she owe him a favor? After all, he'd lit the fuse she'd wanted ignited so much. Really, if she thought about it, she'd ruthlessly used him for sex then shoved him out the door. Definitely very un-Southern-hospitality-like of her.

Her better judgment sternly informed her she was rationalizing, but her heart wasn't listening.

She dialed Jackson's New York office number quickly, before she had time to change her mind.

AFTER LEAVING a message on Riley's voice mail, Jackson replaced the receiver of his office phone in its cradle, then dragged his hands down his face, frustrated and annoyed with himself. He'd known she wouldn't be in her office this late, especially on a Friday night. And the phone call had been completely unnecessary. Yet still he'd made it. Why? So he could hear her damn voice on her voice mail. Good God, how insane was that?

A disgusted sound escaped him, and he snatched up his take-out Thai container and viciously jabbed a shrimp with the end of one chopstick. Popping the savory morsel into his mouth, he frowned and chewed as if he were gnawing on glass, shaking his head at his own inexplicable behavior.

He'd planned to send her his revised budget earlier this week in the hopes that she might have a chance to look it over before leaving for the weekend, but he'd had to wait to get the proper documentation for all the increases he was requesting. Between the waiting and all the interruptions that had conspired to steal his time since returning from Atlanta, he'd been delayed. Now there was no way she could look at it before Monday. Which would give him a valid excuse to call her first thing Monday morning—to reiterate that he needed her approval ASAP.

Oh, sure, his inner voice mocked. *That's why you*

want to call her—to tell her something you've already told her twice.

He lifted some pad Thai noodles to his mouth with the chopsticks and again shook his head, recalling the way his heart had pounded just dialing her number, as if he were some Cupid-struck fifteen-year-old calling his high-school crush. He'd quickly discovered that even the sound of her recorded voice caused a flood of images of her, of them together, to flash through his mind.

The sound of her voice? his inner voice interrupted again. *Oh, sure.* That's *what got you thinking about her. 'Cause you haven't been thinking about her at all for the past week.*

Yeah, right.

Unfortunately, he'd thought of little else. Even when he'd managed to shove her from the foreground of his thoughts, she'd remained firmly embedded in the background, twisting through his brain, interrupting his train of thought so many times he'd given up trying to keep his runaway mind on the track.

They'd exchanged a few e-mails, but she'd kept hers strictly business and he'd forced himself to do the same. It irked and confused him that he'd reached for the phone to call her at least a dozen times, spent more hours than he cared to admit trying to fabricate a valid reason to phone her. In the end, he'd settled for e-mail—until tonight, when he'd finally given in to the plaguing urge.

But here it was, four days since they'd seen each other, and he hadn't been able to erase her from his mind *at all.* The feel of her in his arms, wrapped around him, the taste of her kiss, the sweet, vanilla scent of her skin, the silkiness of her hair had all burrowed into his mind and refused to budge, all still startlingly vivid, all still filling him with desire and longing. And lust. Damn it, she'd knocked him on his ass the instant he'd set eyes on her, and he didn't like it, or understand it one bit. He hadn't felt this unsettled and randy since…well, he didn't know when. But somehow he couldn't shake the suspicion that he was feeling more than just randy.

Based on his instantaneous attraction to her, he'd expected the sex to be great, and it had been. Yet he'd experienced great sex before, and it hadn't left him feeling like…this. What he hadn't expected was to be so disarmed by Riley. So charmed. Nothing in her terse e-mails had given him a clue to the warm, passionate woman she'd turned out to be. He'd felt a connection with her that he'd never experienced before, something that went deeper than sex. She'd turned him on—powerfully—but she'd also made him laugh. Made him want to talk to her. Listen to her. Learn all about her. Fall asleep with her. Wake up next to her.

He stabbed another shrimp. Good God, he was losing his mind. And his edge. Damn woman was cluttering up his head and had his synapses all out of whack. Surely once this budget matter was settled he'd be able to stop thinking about her. It was natural that he'd think about her while doing the budget, since he needed to send it to her for approval. But once it was approved, the amount of contact between them would subside substantially. And he could delegate most anything that required contact with the accounting department to one of his senior managers. Yup, once the budget was done, she'd fade from his memory.

His office phone rang and he groaned. Had to be

Brian calling—again. His brother was determined to drag him out to a club tonight even though Jackson had already told him three times he just wasn't in the mood. He reached out and punched the speaker button.

"For the last time, I don't want to go," he yelled around a mouthful of noodles.

A heartbeat of silence, then Riley's throaty, amused voice drifted from the phone. "Oooookay. But I don't recall asking if you *did* want to go."

He heart performed a crazy somersault and he bolted upright in his chair. He hastily swallowed, then caught himself about to straighten his loosened tie—as if she could see him. Man, he really was losing his marbles.

"Jackson...are you there?"

"Yes. Sorry. Thought you were my brother. Hi." *Oh, real smooth, Jackson. You sound like an ass.*

"Hi. Um, how are you?"

Crappy. Out of sorts. And it's all your fault. "Great. How are you?"

"Fine, thanks. I was working late and happened to see your e-mails. About reviewing the revised budget—I'll be out of the office Monday and Tuesday of next week, so if we wait until after the weekend, I won't be able to get to it until Wednesday."

Damn. That would throw off his entire schedule even further. But what had she said? He replayed her words then asked, "What do you mean 'if we wait until after the weekend?'"

"If you're willing to stick around your office for a while in case I have any questions or problems, I'll look at it now."

He stared at the beige phone as if it were an angel of mercy. "You're serious?"

"I am. Is that a yes?"

"Absolutely." He tunneled his fingers through his hair. "This is really great of you."

"I'm sure you don't mean to sound so shocked."

"Well, I *am* surprised. I mean, it's Friday night. I'm sure you have better things to do."

"I'll miss the Braves game on TV. And if you had any inkling what a diehard baseball fan I am, you'd understand the sacrifice."

"Being a diehard tennis fan who hates to miss a televised match, I understand. I'll owe you."

"Big time."

"Consider me in your debt. This is going above and beyond in titanic proportions, and I really appreciate it. Thank you."

"You're welcome. So I'll get busy. Oh—one more thing. I read your e-mail about the planned updates for the Prestige Web site. They sound great. But there're a couple of typos in the memo."

Jackson groaned. "Great. And it's gone out to the entire company. How did they get by me? I reread the memo before I hit Send."

"It happens. I wouldn't even have mentioned it except you'll probably want to correct these particular typos and resend the message."

"Uh-oh. What did I write?" He turned to his computer and called up his word processing program.

"In the first paragraph, second line, I'm guessing it's supposed to read 'with a single *click* of the mouse' as opposed to 'with a single *lick*.'"

The document appeared on Jackson's screen and when his gaze zeroed in on the second line, he cringed. "Oh, man."

A soft laugh came from the phone speaker and he sizzled a frown at it. "It's not funny."

"I know. I'm sorry. It's just that I had this sudden visual of all the Prestige employees touching their PC screens with their tongues. But wait till you see the second typo."

"It can't possibly be any worse."

"'Fraid so. Second paragraph, fourth line. Unless Prestige is heading in an entirely new direction, I think you mean, 'We'll have *six* pages added to the Web site' instead of, 'We'll have *sex* pages added.'"

Jackson stared at the error and dragged his hands down his face. "Damn. It just got worse."

"Lick, sex…hmm. Makes one wonder what you were thinking about when you drafted that memo," she said, the ripe speculation in her voice clearly audible over the speakerphone. "Freudian slips?"

I was thinking about you, if you must know. "Maybe. Maybe I'm just not a great typist. But hey, if you're going to make a typo, make it a beauty—that's my motto."

"Obviously. Why didn't your secretary read it over for you?"

"I told her to take off after lunch. She mentioned that today's her son's second birthday and I wanted her to have the chance to spend the afternoon with him."

"That was nice of you."

"I detect a note of amazement in your voice that I would do something nice. I thought I already proved to you that I'm not always such a bad guy." When she didn't answer right away, he prompted, "Well?"

"I'm thinking."

He could hear the teasing lilt in her voice, and he instantly pictured her, sitting at her desk, her golden brown eyes dancing with mischief. A pang of longing blindsided him, and he forced out a laugh.

"Hardee-har-har. Listen, I really appreciate the heads-up on the mistakes. Now I can fix them and send out a new message with a Correction header before anyone's had a chance to read the lick and sex version."

"Good idea, although I suspect the lick and sex version would make for an interesting start to everyone's Monday. As for finding the typos, no problem. I'm an auditor. It's my job to catch mistakes…speaking of which, let's hope there won't be any in your revised budget or we'll be here all night. I'd better get started on it."

"Right. I'll be here if you have any questions."

"Great. I'll call you later."

She disconnected, and Jackson did the same. Then he leaned back in his chair, clasped his hands behind his head and grinned.

She'd called him. And she was going to call him again later tonight. She hadn't had plans this evening—well, except with the TV, and that didn't count—which answered a question that had plagued him all day: would she have a date tonight? He'd tried to force the disturbing question from his mind because he didn't like the way the thought of her with another guy made him feel.

But she'd sacrificed rooting for the home team for him. And she'd saved him from the embarrassment of his typos. And even though it wasn't wise, he liked the way that made him feel.

The next few hours flew by with drafting memos and digging through the mountain that had accumulated in his inbox. Just after midnight, his phone rang. His heart jumped, and he told himself it was merely because the noise startled him. After pushing the speaker button, he said, "Lange here."

"Jackson, it's Riley. We have a problem."

Damn. "What sort of problem?"

"The numbers don't add up. You've made an error somewhere—either inputted a wrong amount or transposed a number. Or maybe it's a formula error in the spreadsheet. Do you have your original source documents handy?"

"Right here," he said, dragging the sheath of papers toward him.

"Good. Let's start with the travel expenses first and go from there. We'll figure out where the error is."

He complied. Finally, when they were checking the general and administrative expenses, they came across a discrepancy.

"Let's see if that's it," she said, and he imagined her fingers flying over a calculator. Nearly a minute of silence passed before she said, "That's it. Everything adds up now. Make the correction to your spreadsheet, then resend me the file."

"And the budget? Is it approved?"

"On my end, yes. Of course, Paul has to sign off on it, but I can't see any reason why he won't. I'll make sure I forward everything to him, with a high priority flag, before I leave tonight so he can take care of it first thing Monday morning. Congratulations, Jackson. You've got yourself a new budget."

Which brought him one step closer to accomplishing what he'd been hired to do—bring Prestige and Elite together. "Thank you. Have I told you how much I appreciate what you've done tonight?"

"Yes—but some additional genuflecting always makes a girl feel good," she said with a laugh.

"I'm on my knees."

A snortlike sound came from the phone. "You are

not. You're sitting in your comfy chair *telling* me you're on your knees."

"It's the thought that counts. Really, I'm extremely grateful to you for pulling the late night and extra hours to help me. If there's ever anything I can do to return the favor, don't hesitate to ask."

"All right. And don't think I won't collect. I like to keep my debits and credits all balanced. It's the accountant in me." An unmistakable yawn came through the speaker loud and clear. "Get going on resending that file so we can both go home, okay?"

"I'm on it."

"Good. Have a nice weekend."

"Thanks. You, too." Before he could think of a reason not to, Jackson snatched up the receiver and pressed it to his ear. "Riley, wait. How about giving me your e-mail address?"

"You have it, bright boy. You've been shooting annoying messages my way since your first day with the company."

"I meant your personal e-mail." When she hesitated, he quickly added, "My mom forwards me all sorts of jokes and stuff she gets from her friends. Yesterday, she forwarded a recipe that might interest you."

"Your mom sends you recipes? I thought you weren't much of a cook."

"I'm not, but she has high hopes and tries to encourage me. You know, so I don't starve to death or eat doughnuts for dinner."

"We're not supposed to eat doughnuts for dinner?" He smiled at the exaggerated shock in her voice. "Uh-oh. Nobody ever told me that. So what's this recipe for?"

"The Most Incredible Fudge Brownies on Planet Earth."

Her sharp intake of breath reminded him of the erotic sound she made just before her orgasm overtook her. "Oh, my."

He shifted in his seat. "According to the ladies in Mom's canasta club, they're aptly named. If you give me your e-mail address, I'll forward it along."

"Sold. It's WillWork4Chocolate@SweetStuff.com."

He wrote it down on a sticky note then smiled. "Cute address."

"And very apt. Just don't mention to Marcus or Paul that I'm willing to work for chocolate, okay?"

"Hmm, I don't know. I'm thinking that replacing your salary with a few pounds of candy would save the company a bundle. I'd think a financial gal such as yourself would appreciate that."

"Yes, you'd think," she said, sounding disgruntled. "You know, I heard a very sad story about a marketing executive who ratted out a co-worker. Horrible, grisly tale."

He laughed. "I'll keep that in mind."

"Good. Keep this in mind, too—if you don't deliver on that recipe, consider your next three expense reports denied. Now go send me that corrected file."

"Will do. Good night, Sweet Stuff."

"Ha, ha. G'night."

He replaced the receiver and couldn't contain his smile as he looked down at the sticky note bearing her e-mail address.

Now all he needed to do was come up with a brownie recipe.

7

THE FOLLOWING Wednesday evening, Riley was shoving folders into her briefcase when Gloria hailed her from her office doorway.

"Hey, Riley. Haven't seen you since lunch last Friday. How are you?"

Riley glanced up from her task and smiled at her friend. "Good. I was out meeting with property managers Monday and Tuesday, and today has just been insane. I can't wait to get home, plop in front of the TV and relax. Braves game is on tonight. How about you?"

"Also on my way out." Gloria struck a dramatic pose against the doorjamb, then whispered loudly, "I have a D-A-T-E."

"Great. Who's the lucky man?"

"Remember the gorgeous guy I told you about who lives in my apartment complex? The tennis pro? The one with the great legs?"

"How could I forget? You've talked about him for weeks," Riley teased. "But I thought he had a girlfriend."

"*Had* being the operative word. I ran into him at the supermarket over the weekend—I mean literally ran into him with my basket in the produce department."

"Accidentally?"

She shrugged. "Accidentally on purpose. Anyway, we started talking, one thing led to another, and we're having dinner together tonight at the new Mexican cantina that opened on Peachtree. Fajitas, margaritas and luscious man—my favorite."

Riley chuckled. She shifted her purse onto her shoulder, grabbed her overstuffed briefcase, and they headed toward the elevators. "Even though dinner with a luscious man can't beat leftover pizza, ratty sweats and a televised baseball game, I hope you have a great time. Don't do anything I wouldn't do."

Gloria adopted an angelically innocent expression. "Shouldn't be a problem, considering that you indulged in wild sex with the last gorgeous man you met. How is Mr. Lange, by the way?"

Riley forced her expression to remain impassive, but she suspected Gloria would see the blush she felt heating her cheeks. She quickly brought Gloria up to date on last Friday's late-night budget session, concluding with, "So I gave him my private e-mail address."

"And has he been in touch?"

"Yes. On Sunday, he sent me the brownie recipe he promised."

Gloria smiled. "Ah. A man of his word. Was it perhaps accompanied by a flirty message?"

"No. Just, 'Hope you enjoy the brownies,' which, if I'm absolutely honest, sort of disappointed me. I mean, not that I wanted or expected him to come on strong, but—"

"But a girl likes a little flirting," Gloria agreed.

"But then on Monday..." Riley paused as they passed through the heavy glass doors.

Gloria jabbed the elevator's Down button. "What happened Monday?"

"A delivery was waiting for me when I got home from work."

"Ooh. Flowers?"

"A gorgeous bouquet of flowers *and* a refrigerated box of Boston Cream doughnuts, shipped from his favorite bakery in New York, accompanied by a very nice note thanking me for staying late to help him Friday night." Heat rose in Riley's cheeks as she recalled her favorite line of that note: *Wanted you to try what were the best Boston Creams ever—until the ones we shared together took over the number one spot. But these run a close second.*

"Very nice," Gloria said, waving her hand in front of her face and pretending to swoon. "Wonder if Rob the tennis pro will turn out to be that romantic?" Before Riley could reply, Gloria rushed on, "Oh, who cares? He looks so good on a tennis court, he doesn't need to be romantic." Riley instantly recalled that Jackson was a tennis fan. Hmm. He, too, would look outstanding on a tennis court—

"So did you e-mail Jackson?"

Gloria's question yanked her attention back. The elevator opened and they stepped into the car, then Riley pushed the *L* button. After the doors closed, she answered, "Yes, to thank him for the flowers and the doughnuts."

"And?"

"And as of last night, I haven't heard back from him."

"I'd lay odds you'll have a message when you get home tonight. The man is definitely interested."

"The man was simply thanking me for saving his butt."

"He's fascinated with you."

A thrill she firmly ignored rippled through Riley

at Gloria's words. "He lives nine hundred miles away."

"Can you say *frequent flyer miles?*"

"We have completely divergent interests."

"So? Rob's a tennis pro and under no circumstances could I ever be described as an athlete." She waggled her brows. "Actually I hope he'll suggest some private lessons."

"He's a demanding pest at work." But even as the words passed Riley's lips, she had to admit that that description of Jackson wasn't as dead-on as it once had been.

"But he's improving," Gloria said, echoing Riley's thoughts.

"True..." He was definitely ambitious, but ambition, as opposed to laziness, was a trait she'd always admired. And Marcus, who was a brilliant man, obviously thought highly of Jackson's abilities or he never would have hired him.

The elevator opened and they made their way to the parking garage. "I'm parked over there," Riley said, nodding toward the right. "Have a great time tonight. Can't wait to hear all about it."

"Hope there's lots to tell," Gloria said with a devilish grin. "And don't forget to check your e-mail."

Riley waved and headed toward her car. Don't forget to check her e-mail? No, forgetting would not present a problem. But she suspected that the eagerness eating at her to do so might eventually turn into a problem.

Thanks to the Atlanta traffic, which was even worse than usual, it took Riley over an hour to arrive home. After dropping her purse and briefcase in the cream ceramic-tiled foyer, she flipped through the mail as she made her way toward her bedroom, resisting the overwhelming urge to make a beeline for her laptop and check her e-mail. No, she was in control. She could wait until after she'd changed her clothes and stuck her pizza in the oven.

She spied a note on the snack bar and scanned Tara's words that she was going to dinner and a late movie with her friend Lynda and would spend the night at Lynda's house. Riley nodded with satisfaction and continued toward her bedroom. It had taken a lot of arguing, work and patience to get Tara to write such notes, telling Riley where she was going and if she planned to stay out all night, but Riley wouldn't let up. She'd spent too many nights worrying about Tara's whereabouts, whether her headstrong sister was safe or dead in an alley somewhere. Riley extended that courtesy to Tara and she expected it in return. The fact that Tara now left the notes—even though she still considered it 'juvenile'—was a hard-earned victory.

After quickly changing into her sweats and favorite Braves T-shirt, she returned to the family room where she flicked on the TV. The game wasn't scheduled to start for another ten minutes, so she turned on the oven and snatched a soft drink from the fridge. After she'd taken a long, chilled swig, her gaze fell on her laptop sitting on the oak coffee table in the family room. As a matter of pride, she forced herself to take another two sips of soda before approaching the laptop. Settling herself on the sofa, she booted up, then clicked onto her e-mail.

There was a message from Jackson. Sent less than thirty minutes ago.

A flutter of excited anticipation tingled through her and she quickly opened the note.

Glad you liked the flowers and doughnuts. Bought some for myself (doughnuts, not flowers), but due to mother-inspired guilt will not eat one until *after* dinner, although I suspect Mom would be horrified if she knew dinner was going to be leftover pizza. Hope your day was better than mine, Sweet Stuff.

Something inside Riley went all warm and gooey with longing at the short note, and she instantly pictured him, flopped onto a comfortable sofa, munching on a slice of reheated pizza, trying to forget about a stressful day at the office. Tired. Alone.

Sort of like her. Actually, *exactly* like her.

She clicked on the Reply key and her fingers flew across the keyboard.

Must be something in the air since I'm having leftover pizza tonight, too. But no complaints—it's my favorite thing to eat while watching a ball game and tonight's match up against the Mets promises to be good. Don't suppose you plan to watch the game, Tennis-Boy? Will fire up the espresso machine and make a latte to complement a Boston Cream during the seventh inning stretch. You think you had a bad day? Ha! Beat this— in spite of hiding my doughnuts behind a withered head of lettuce and some limp carrots in the veggie drawer of the fridge, Tara managed to find them and snagged not one but *two* of my precious stash. I've taken her out of my will. And when I bake those Best Brownies on Planet Earth, I'm going to tie her to a chair and make her watch me eat the entire pan by myself.

Riley hesitated, debated, chewed on her lip for several seconds, then gave in to the urge and typed one final line:

If you decide to tune in the game and want to hear me gloat about how badly the Braves are whupping your New York team, give me a call.

She typed her phone number, then quickly hit the Send key before she changed her mind. Then she resolutely stood and marched to the fridge, trying not to think of the questions bouncing through her mind.

Would he call her? Did she really want him to?

Yes, she hoped he would. And yes, she really wanted him to.

She'd just popped the pizza in the oven and set the timer, and was reaching for the remote to up the muted volume as the game was about to start, when the phone rang.

Could it be him? Surely not. She'd only sent her e-mail a few minutes ago. Still, her heart skipped crazily and she forced herself to count three rings before she picked up. "Hello?"

"So what toppings do you like on your pizza?"

A heated tingle consumed her entire body at the sound of his deep voice, and she knew that if she looked in a mirror, she'd see an idiotic smile plastered across her face.

"Who is this?" she asked in a husky drawl.

"Tennis-Boy, although I think I'd prefer Tennis-*Man*. And don't try to tell me that you're not Sweet Stuff, because, Riley…I would recognize your voice *anywhere*."

Her knees developed a sudden aversion to standing at the sexy, intimate timbre in his voice, and she plopped into one of the oak kitchen chairs. "Er, good to know."

"So, what's on your pizza?" he asked again.

Damned if she could remember. And he had a lot

of nerve asking her these darn complicated questions when he'd just dissolved her knees. She mentally shook herself and, shooting her gaze over to the oven, her memory kicked in. "Veggies. Onions, mushrooms, tomatoes, broccoli."

"You put *broccoli* on your pizza? That's...sacrilegious."

"You don't like broccoli—why am I not surprised?"

"Actually, I do like broccoli. Just not on my pizza."

"Aha. So you're one of those fussy eaters."

He laughed. "Fussy? Are you kidding? You're talking to a guy who survived an entire semester of college almost exclusively on SpaghettiOs and has eaten a frozen dinner that was cooked in the fireplace over a Duraflame log."

Riley shook her head and chuckled. "What would possess you to cook a frozen dinner in the fireplace?"

"It was actually my mother's idea. I was in high school at the time and the electricity was out, so no oven. We all grabbed a dinner out of the freezer and made an evening out of it. Worst-tasting thing I ever ate—half charred, half frozen, but definitely one of the most fun meals I've ever had." The deep rumble of his laugh came through the receiver, tickling her ear. "The house smelled really funky for weeks after that."

An image of him, sitting in front of a fireplace, laughing, poking at a foil-covered dinner rose in Riley's mind, suffusing her with a longing she couldn't name other than to know that she wished she'd shared that evening with him. "Sounds like a fun time."

"It was."

"So...I'm guessing you prefer your pizza smothered with artery-clogging sausage and pepperoni."

"Yup. To go along with the artery-clogging extra

cheese. But I prefer to think of it as my daily allowance of protein and dairy."

She couldn't help but smile. "I bet you do. Same way I call the nuts in brownies protein and the milk in chocolate dairy."

He chuckled. "Works for me."

"So I take it this phone call means that you're going to tune into the game and let me gloat when the Braves wipe up the field with the Mets."

"No way. I'm watching tennis with my pizza. The men's second round matches are coming up."

"Yippee."

"At least it's not boring. Watching baseball is like waiting for paint to dry. Just a bunch of overpaid guys standing around waiting for the ball to come to them."

"Oh, yeah, and those tennis players earn minimum wage, I'm sure. At least in baseball they do more than just *hit* the ball."

"At least tennis *moves*. You could fall asleep waiting for something to happen during a baseball game."

"At least you don't need a chiropractor after watching baseball. None of that monotonous back, forth, back, forth."

"It's good neck exercise."

"Right. Because my neck needs a whole lot of exercise."

"You really need to start thinking outside the box more, Addison."

"And you need to realize that if you step too far outside the box, there's nothing under your feet except dead air space."

"I guess we'll just need to agree to disagree about this. Actually I called because I was just now thinking about you."

Her fingers tightened on the receiver. "Oh? What were you thinking?"

A few heartbeats of silence followed her question. Then he asked in a low, serious voice, "Do you really want to know?"

No. "Yes."

"I was thinking about your smile. Your laugh. The decadent, sexy way you eat a doughnut. The delicious vanilla scent of your skin. The way your hands, your mouth felt on me. The way my hands, my mouth felt on you."

Her eyes slid closed at his quiet words, evoking a parade of sensual images of them together that were permanently seared into her brain. It was a darn good thing she was sitting down; otherwise she would slither to the floor in a boneless heap.

"Actually," he continued in that same husky voice, "it's not accurate to say I was 'just now' thinking about you. The truth is, I haven't stopped thinking about you. Not since the minute I walked into that fortune-teller's tent."

Riley's heart pounded so hard she could hear the thumping in her ears. Deep down, she knew he'd said exactly what she'd hoped he would, but she hadn't expected him to say it. And he hadn't pulled any punches—just told her. He'd thrown her a perfect curveball. Now she needed to decide if she wanted to swing at it. When she'd abandoned her "dull" shroud, she'd been ready to do something daring. But with Jackson she'd gotten a lot more than she'd bargained for. She hadn't envisioned indulging in a full-blown affair, especially with a man she'd only recently referred to as the Bane of her Existence. But she'd been spectacularly unsuccessful in forgetting him. His forthright honesty compelled her to respond in kind.

"I...I've thought about you, as well."

"Good. Hate to think I'm suffering alone."

"What makes you think I'm suffering?"

"If you're not, don't tell me. It makes me feel better to think of you being as miserable as I am."

"Wow. You entice many women with smooth lines like that?"

"I'm not much on smooth lines—"

"Obviously."

"—because that's all they are—lines. Games. I've dished out my fair share and been on the receiving end of them enough times to have developed a real dislike of them. I'd rather toss the unvarnished truth onto the table and let the chips fall where they may. At least then I haven't done anything to tarnish my integrity."

Shame filled Riley because even though she liked to think that she would have been as upfront in admitting her feelings, she knew she would have sidestepped the issue if he hadn't said the words first. Which made her a card-carrying member of The Chicken Club, an organization from which she'd prefer to resign. Right now. But resurrecting the pre-Tara Riley was proving more difficult than she'd anticipated. Clearly old habits died hard. And why was this all so...confusing? It was supposed to be easy—have fun, be daring, recapture her youth. Yet nothing was going as she'd planned.

"I appreciate the honesty and didn't mean to sound otherwise. My only defense is that I found it...startling."

"That I would be honest? Gee, thanks." There was no missing the underlying hurt in his voice.

"I'm sorry," she said, and really meant it. "I'm saying this badly. It's just that until I actually met you, I have to admit that I really disliked you."

"I see. Well, I guess I'm guilty of the same thing with you. But I don't dislike you anymore, Riley. And I'm the first to admit that I sometimes say things badly, so let me try again. What I *meant* was that I'm encouraged that you've thought of me, and I hope it's been in the same way that I've been thinking about you." He paused, then asked softly, "Has it?"

She wanted to lie, and maybe if he'd only crossed her mind once or twice, she might have been able to do so. "I can't deny that I've thought of our night together." Then, wanting, needing to steer this conversation onto a safer path—before she admitted just how much she'd thought of him and that night—she adopted a light tone and added, "But I've also thought about how little we have in common, a fact hammered home again by our choice of TV viewing this evening and our diametrically opposed tastes in pizza toppings."

"I bet if we tried really hard, we could find something we have in common."

Feeling on more solid ground, Riley rose, clicked the phone to speaker mode, then checked on her pizza. "I think we'd have to dig pretty deep."

"Nah," Jackson said, his deep voice now filling the room. "Hey, here's one—we both have two ears, two eyes and a nose."

"That's ridiculous," Riley said, sliding her pizza from the oven. "We both also have ten fingers, ten toes and—"

"Tongues," he said. "We both have tongues."

"I was going to say 'a mouth,'" she said in her best prim schoolmarm tone.

"And you know how to use yours very well, I might add."

She had to clamp her lips together to keep from laughing, all while a scorching wave of heat rushed through her that had nothing to do with the fact that she'd just opened the oven. "No more body parts in common," she said. "I meant real stuff."

"Hmm. Sounds to me like you're changing the rules midstream, but I'll still play. How's this? We both have business degrees."

"True. But in different areas."

"Ah, now you're just splitting hairs," he said, and she could clearly visualize his triumphant grin... strands of silky, dark hair spilling onto his forehead.

She slid a generous, cheese-oozing slice of pizza onto her plate, snagged a bottle of water from the fridge and plopped herself down at the breakfast bar.

"Not splitting hairs," she said. "Just pointing out that accounting is nothing like *marketing*." She jokingly said the word as if it smelled bad.

"You're right. *Marketing* isn't *boring*," he said, perfectly mimicking her tone.

"Just something else we don't have in common. I find accounting *fascinating*."

"Yeah, well, that's something we *have* in common because I find stuff fascinating, too. Like the way your eyelids get droopy when you're aroused."

Riley sucked in a sharp breath. The light, teasing camaraderie of the past few minutes evaporated like a puff of steam, replaced with a tension and heat she could feel right through the phone line. It was the second time he'd thrown her off balance, and she firmly resolved to get this chat back on track.

"FYI—*droopy* is not a good word to use when describing a woman."

"Thanks for the tip, but I wasn't describing a woman, I was describing your eyelids."

"Which are attached to me, and I'm a woman."

He laughed, then groaned. "Okay, this is one of those girl-trap, 'Does this make my butt look fat?' things that a guy has no chance of winning. Bottom line, Miss Accountant, is that there is nothing droopy about you, and I think your eyelids are sexy when you're aroused."

Riley's nipples hardened at his words, at the intimate tone of his voice, and she grabbed a paper napkin to fan herself. *Speaking of aroused...*

"So, what are you wearing?" he asked.

Oh, no. She wasn't going there. "My oldest Braves T-shirt, complete with the faded mustard stain from last year's opening day game; my rattiest sweats, complete with a hole in the right knee and frayed cuffs; and my favorite yellow fuzzy slippers that, unfortunately, are no longer yellow or very fuzzy."

He laughed. "Where were you the day they mailed out the Victoria's Secret catalogues? Your answer was supposed to give me a visual of skimpy, lacy stuff. Boy, you're not good at this game."

"Ah, but I thought you said you didn't like to play games."

"There are certain games I like to play. You telling me that you're wearing something fantasy-inducing is one of them."

"Well, you're out of luck tonight unless ratty sweats turn you on. So what are *you* wearing?"

"Ratty sweats."

She laughed. "And some old sweatshirt with the

sleeves ripped off, and a pair of gym socks with a hole in the heel, I'll bet."

"Hey, what have you got—a Webcam?"

If only. An eyeful of Jackson in his ratty sweats sounded really…scrumptious. "Nope. I just know how guys like to dress once the suit and tie are ditched. So, any news on the Elite merger—or can't you say?"

"No news yet. Just a lot of continued meetings and schmoozing. Expensive restaurant schmoozing, so brace your frugal self for the expense reports soon to be headed your way. Marcus is flying into New York tomorrow, so there'll be more meetings and more restaurants."

"I'll see if I can arrange a bank loan, Sir Spend-thrift," she said in a dust-dry tone.

"Good idea. There's also talk of another big project coming up. All in all, more than enough to keep me busy. So, do you have any exciting plans this weekend?"

"If you consider helping Tara pack boxes for her move exciting, then I have a doozy of a weekend planned."

"When is she moving?"

"The following weekend. For the first time in five years I'll have my apartment all to myself." She blew out a long breath. "That sounds so…liberating. What about you—any big plans?"

"A party Saturday night to celebrate the folks' thirty-fifth wedding anniversary."

Riley smiled. "That's great. An amazing accomplishment."

"According to my mom and dad, the secret to a successful marriage is marrying the right person."

A jolt of nostalgia hit her. "My parents had a similar philosophy—you can't win if you don't pick the right teammate."

A soft beep sounded, and he said, "That's my call waiting. Can you hold on a sec?"

"Sure."

He came back on the line a few seconds later and said, "My sister Shelley is on the line and there's some sort of snag with the anniversary party arrangements. She's pregnant, her husband's out of town, and she's ready to rip out her hair. I'm sorry, but I need to get going and do some damage control."

"No problem. Good luck solving your party problem."

"Thanks. Oh, and Riley, don't start your gloating too soon. During the tennis match's commercial break, I flipped over to the baseball game and noted that the Mets are ahead six-zero in the third inning. 'Night." He chuckled in a distinctly evil fashion then disconnected.

Riley's gaze flew to the TV screen. With the volume on mute, she'd completely forgotten about the game. After grabbing the remote, she upped the sound and stared at the score.

Well, damn.

With a frown, she picked up her pizza and took a bite, noting that while her meal was now barely warm, she was filled with an unaccustomed heat. And an unsettling disquiet. And it was all because of him. His sexy voice. His sexy laugh. His sexy reminders of the night they'd spent together. A night the likes of which her body desperately longed for an encore performance.

But why, oh why, did Jackson Lange have to be the man her hormones were screaming for? While it was true that their working relationship had improved a bit, she didn't doubt for one minute that their current cautious détente would eventually give way to more clashes. And there was no forgetting the nine hundred miles that separated them. They'd shared a night together and that was all. Over and done. She needed to forget and move on. She *wanted* to forget and move on.

However, forgetting the feel of him, the taste of him, wasn't proving easy, and she mentally thunked herself on the head for giving him her phone number. What had she been thinking? Well, even if she couldn't forget him right now, she would eventually. And in the meantime, she'd concentrate on moving on. After Tara left and Riley's home was once again her own, she was going to throw a party. Live it up. Recapture the bachelorette-type fun she'd enjoyed before Tara had moved in. Date up a storm. Hit the clubs. Meet lots of interesting men—men with whom she shared similar interests. Men with whom it was not a doomed-to-failure case of opposites attracting. Men who did not require a visit to the airport to date.

Yes, she was a planner and that was the plan. Somewhere in the back of her mind she could almost hear Gloria advising her to come up with a Plan B, but she managed, with a great deal of effort, to ignore it.

8

ONE WEEK after their first phone conversation, one week after the Mets had clobbered the Braves eleven to three, Jackson slapped off his alarm clock and glared at the digital numbers informing him it was time to get his butt out of bed and get ready for work. He rolled over onto his back, squeezed his eyes shut and growled at the untimely interruption of his sleep—not so much because he was still tired, but because he'd been having a dream. A really great dream. He and Riley, naked, her hands skimming over him, her breasts filling his palms, his erection gliding deep inside her. His body throbbed and, opening one eye, he looked down and groaned at the tented sheet draped over his arousal. Not that he was surprised. He'd awakened in the same condition every morning since he'd met her, which he supposed was to be expected since she continued to fill every corner of his mind—waking and sleeping.

For the past six mornings, Jackson had started his day by sending an e-mail to Riley's personal address containing an accountant joke. She'd replied each time with a marketing joke. He'd also called her at home twice—on the only two nights he'd gotten home himself at a reasonable hour. They'd spent over an hour on the phone each time, trading verbal spars, talking about their lives, childhoods, families, travels and experiences. He'd started off both conversations by teasingly asking her what she was wearing, and both times she'd laughed and given him the same answer of ratty sweats and old T-shirt. "Some day I'm going to call and catch you dressed in something slinky," he'd warned with a chuckle.

Aside from the fact that she didn't lounge around in lingerie, he'd learned she loved to cook, hated doing laundry, desperately wanted a dog but planned to wait until she owned a house and had a yard, loved the beach and had never tried downhill skiing. After he'd revealed that he was a miserable cook, didn't mind doing laundry, had never had a dog growing up because his mom was allergic, loved the beach and went skiing every winter, they'd both laughed.

"At least we both like the beach," he'd said.

She'd replied, "Right. One out of fifty or so things must set some sort of incompatibility record."

While they didn't have a lot in common as far as everyday things were concerned, he was starting to sense that they might agree on several deeper issues. Already it was clear that family was important to both of them. Was it possible that they shared similar views on other important issues as well? Maybe. One thing was certain—they were very compatible sexually.

Pushing out a long breath, Jackson clasped his hands behind his head and closed his eyes. The images of Riley he'd been unable to banish filled his mind and his jaw tightened. Damn it, it was ridiculous the way this woman haunted him. Yeah, the sex had been great, but this was crazy. Was the night they'd spent together really as magical as he thought, or had he just somehow built it up in his mind? Was it possible that he'd enjoyed her so much because he hadn't been with anyone for a while?

But he couldn't deny that more than his body and libido were involved here—she'd also taken over his mind and he wasn't sure he liked it. He knew all too well that sparks fizzled out, and the hotter the spark, the faster the fizzle-out. But this spark hadn't died. In fact, with every phone call and e-mail, it seemed to burn brighter. The question was, what did he intend to do about it? If a relocation to Atlanta was a done deal, that question wouldn't present such difficulties. But there was a chance the merger might not happen. And even if it did, the question of possibly relocating could be complicated by the job interview he had scheduled this afternoon. For an executive position with Winthrop Hotels at their home office in New York. Exactly the sort of position he'd been busting his ass to earn a shot at. Winthrop's CEO had called him yesterday to request the meeting, and Jackson had jumped at the chance. He'd considered telling Riley about it, but had just as quickly decided against it. No point in bringing up something that might not amount to anything. If it developed into an issue, he'd tell her.

And speaking of Riley, did he have an e-mail from her?

The question was enough to propel him from the bed to make his way to the kitchen, where he booted up his laptop, which sat in the corner of the small breakfast bar. Early morning sunshine filtered through the window, spreading shafts of golden warmth over the pale oak cabinets and forest-green countertops. While he waited, he snagged his favorite ceramic mug, which looked like a bright yellow tennis ball, and poured himself a cup of strong coffee while performing his morning ritual of silently thanking the genius who had invented the programmable coffeepot. After enjoying that first bracing sip, he popped a bagel into the toaster, then hitched one hip onto the oak barstool and clicked onto his e-mail.

Four new messages—from Mom, Shelley, Brian and Riley. His heart rate kicked up a notch when he saw Riley's name, but he decided to save her note for last. Mom's message was short, just wanting to let him know that she'd talked to Aunt Sophie last night and Aunt Sophie's neighbor's daughter-in-law's friend from Jersey was single and looking and would *love* to meet him, and was he available this weekend to have dinner with her?

Yikes. Jackson grimaced and quickly clicked on Brian's message.

Hey dude, dropped by to see the folks last night. Wanted to give you a heads-up that Mom was in a serious powwow with Aunt Sophie and you were the main topic of conversation. Seems there's some chick in Jersey who's just "perfect" for you. You know what that means—extended out-of-town business trip! Good luck, man. Better you than me! Later, bro.

Jackson typed a quick reply to Brian:

Understand Jersey girl has sister. I'm sure Mom would be happy to arrange a double date.

With a brotherly smirk, he hit Send, then opened Shelley's message, which she'd sent to the entire family, telling everyone that she'd rescheduled her monthly sonogram from tomorrow until Saturday because Dave had to remain out of town for an extra day and she didn't want "daddy" to miss going with her to the doctor, especially since they'd decided to find out the sex of the baby on this visit. Jackson's jaw tightened as he read between the lines on that one, knowing Shelley needed her husband's support during those monthly visits. After Shelley'd suffered two miscarriages in the past two years, the entire family anxiously awaited the results of her monthly sonogram. He typed off a short, cheery note telling her to rest and that he couldn't wait to know if he needed to start buying Barbies or G.I. Joes. He hit Send again, then opened Riley's message.

How many marketing executives does it take to change a light bulb?

One to change the bulb, and forty-nine to say, "I could have done that!"

Hope you have a good day. BTW, for a think-outside-the-box guy who says accountants are boring, your JTLange@JTLange.com e-mail address is pretty ho-hum. What does the *T* in 'JTLange' stand for anyway?

A smile curved Jackson's lips and he immediately typed a reply:

How many accountants does it take to change a light bulb?

Two. One to change the light bulb and one to check that it was done within the given budget.

Hope you have a good day. BTW, you only think my address is boring because you don't remember what the *T* stands for. I told you my middle name was Trouble....

He hit Send, then with a grin, picked up his coffee mug and headed toward the bathroom to shower, pleased that he'd come to a decision regarding a nagging question. *You won't think I'm ho-hum the next time we meet, Miss Addison,* he thought, turning on the spray. He would no longer even consider the possibility that they wouldn't see each other again. He needed to know, *had* to know, if that initial magic they'd shared could be repeated. They would definitely meet again. He intended to see to it. And if his morning meeting with Paul Stanfield and several other Prestige executives regarding the new project they'd discussed went as well as he believed it would, he and Riley would be seeing each other very soon.

WOULD HE call her tonight?

The question echoed through Riley's mind for what had to be the dozenth—okay, two dozenth—time that day as she struggled to balance her purse, laptop case and two grocery bags while unlocking her apartment door. As soon as she entered the foyer, she bumped the door closed with her hip, slid the dead bolt home, then hurried through the obstacle course of Tara's packed boxes to the cheery blue and yellow kitchen, where she plopped her parcels on the ocean-colored countertop. A note scrawled in Tara's handwriting was propped against the coffee maker, informing Riley that some college friends were throwing Tara a going-away party at their apartment and since she didn't want to drive home, she planned to spend the night.

With a twinge of guilt pinching her at the relief she felt at having the entire evening to herself, Riley's gaze then flicked to the phone; the unblinking message light indicated no one had called.

Would he call tonight?

"Argh!" She shook her head and looked at the ceiling, totally frustrated with herself for allowing the question to crawl into her mind yet again. What did she care if he called? In fact, she hoped he wouldn't. She planned to enjoy her solitary evening and revel in the peace and quiet afforded by Tara's absence. She'd cook up a delicious pasta primavera dinner, indulge in a long, hot bubble bath, then curl up with the sports magazine she'd tossed into her cart at the supermarket.

But first, she had to check her e-mail.

After a week of practically pouncing on her PC the minute she walked in the door, she didn't bother to deny—much as she might want to—that she eagerly looked forward to reading the goofy accountant jokes Jackson had been sending her. She pulled up her mail and scanned through the twelve new messages, making a mental note to update her spam blocker because really her penis did not need enlarging as nine of the messages suggested.

Of the three remaining non-penis-enlarging messages, one was from Gloria who'd been in Dallas at a conference this week, and the other two were from Jackson. As a matter of pride, she deliberately clicked first on Gloria's message. Her friend's cheery note said simply, "Conference was great. Indulged in an awesome facial at Neiman's. Let's have lunch tomorrow."

Drawing a deep breath, she clicked on the first of Jackson's e-mails. Still laughing at the light bulb accountant joke and the my-middle-name-is-Trouble reminder, she clicked open his second note.

Since it was recently brought to my attention that my e-mail address was "ho-hum," I am writing to inform you of my new address that is more expressive of my personality. It's TennisMan@OutsideTheBox.com. Greatly looking forward to demonstrating to you that boring was an inaccurate word choice.

Riley's brows hiked up and anticipation curled through her. Demonstrating? Hmm. That sounded intriguing. What did he have in mind? She decided she'd ponder the possibilities while preparing her dinner. After changing into a turquoise tank top and jean shorts, she hit the kitchen and soon the fragrant aroma of sautéing vegetables filled the air, accompanied by background music from her favorite classic rock CD. She shook her hips to the beat, chopping parsley and basil, stirring spaghetti, loving the relaxation that always slipped over her when she cooked, and all the while wondering how Jackson planned to demonstrate that he wasn't boring. She already knew he wasn't, but heck, if he felt the need to prove it, bring it on.

While she enjoyed her pasta, her mind conjured up possible scenarios. Would he send her more flowers? More doughnuts? Sexy e-mails? Make more frequent phone calls? Her gaze drifted to the mockingly silent phone and she stuck her tongue out at it. "Ring, damn it!"

A shrill ring sounded and Riley almost jumped out of her skin. It rang again, proving the first ring was no figment of her imagination and making her wonder what might have happened if she'd said *spit out a million bucks* instead of *ring*.

Heart pounding and breathing hard, she lifted the receiver. "Hello?"

"Riley, it's Jackson. You okay?"

The fact that it was him did nothing to calm her racing heart. "I'm fine."

"You sound…out of breath."

"And you sound like you're in a tunnel."

"I'm on my cell. Is this a bad time?"

"No. I just finished dinner." Now that her heart had settled down—mostly—she ambled to the sofa and plopped down on the overstuffed cream and navy blue striped cushions.

"Do you have plans this evening?"

"As a matter of fact, I do."

"Oh." He paused, then asked, "A date?"

"Yes. A hot date. In my bathtub, with the latest edition of *Sports Weekly* magazine and a glass of wine."

"Ah. A *solo* date." There was no mistaking the relief in his voice, and she couldn't help the feminine satisfaction that ran through her at the knowledge that he was glad her date wasn't with a man.

"Solo," she agreed. "When it comes to *Sports Weekly*, I'm sharing impaired."

"Sweetheart, if I saw you in the tub with that magazine, you wouldn't need to worry about sharing it because reading would be the *last* thing on *my* mind, and I'd do everything I could to make sure it became the last thing on *your* mind as well."

Well, hell, if he were in the tub with her, he wouldn't have to do much to make her forget about reading. Just the mere thought of that scenario hardened her nipples. Clearing her throat, she said lightly, "Since you're over nine hundred miles away, I guess we don't need to worry about that."

"About those nine hundred miles… I had a meeting with Paul Stanfield this morning about a possible new construction project for Prestige in your fair city. It looks like I might need to make another business trip to Atlanta."

Yippee, yelled her hormones. *Hooray,* chimed in her heart. "Oh? When?"

"Soon. So...if I did come to Atlanta, would you maybe invite me over?"

"Depends. Would you bring doughnuts?"

"Absolutely."

"Then I'd think about it."

"What if I promised a sixty-forty split on the doughnuts?"

"I'd get the sixty percent?" she asked, her voice ripe with suspicion.

He laughed. "Yes. And I'd even throw in a long, slow, deep, wet 'hello' kiss."

Whew. A tidal wave of heat swamped her and she vividly recalled how good he was at those long, slow, deep, wet kisses. Hell, she'd have jumped on the kiss offer even without the added bonus of the doughnuts, not that it was necessary to tell *him* that. "Weeeeelll," she said, as if the matter required a great deal of thought, "I guess in that case, I'd invite you over."

Just then her doorbell chime sounded, and she said, "Can you hold on a second? Someone's at my door."

"No problem."

Riley walked to the door then opened it. And stared.

Jackson stood outside, bathed in the glow of the outdoor lights that illuminated the grounds and parking area, a cell phone pressed to his ear. Dressed in a dark suit, a white dress shirt, top button undone, red paisley silk tie loosened, the hint of a five o'clock shadow shading his jaw, he looked tall, strong, masculine, slightly rumpled and altogether delicious. A wheeled suitcase rested next to him. In his other hand, he held a bakery bag.

He smiled, then said into his cell phone, "Hi. Thanks for the invite."

She opened her mouth to speak, only to discover that her jaw had already dropped. Not that it mattered, since she'd somehow forgotten how to form words. That same rush of attraction, of heat and lust, that had consumed her the first time she'd laid eyes on him zoomed through her again, stealing her ability to think—except for the obvious phrase, "You're here," which she managed to speak into her phone.

"I am." He flipped his phone closed, slipped it into his jacket pocket then lifted the paper bag to waggle it at eye level. "Me and the doughnuts."

"But how?"

"Airplane. And some help finding your address courtesy of the Internet reverse phone directory. I did tell you that it looked like I might need to make another business trip to Atlanta."

"That was thirty seconds ago! Obviously your trip is more than a 'might need to.'"

"True."

Her gaze flicked down his suitcase. "And you've obviously just arrived from the airport."

"True again. I guess I could have checked into the hotel first then called you, but…" His words trailed off and the hunger in his eyes tingled warmth down her spine.

"But what?"

"But I wanted to surprise you."

"You did."

"Not unpleasantly, I hope."

Good God, there was nothing unpleasant about it, except maybe for the way her heart threatened to pop out of her shirt and go splat on the cement. "No."

"And I also didn't want to wait that long to see you."

The quietly spoken admission curled tendrils of heat around her, making her feel as if she stood in a sauna.

"How long will you be staying in town?"

"Definitely the rest of this week, and I'm estimating most of, if not all of, next week." His gaze shifted over her shoulder into her apartment. "You plan to make good on your invite and ask me in?"

His question roused Riley from the slack-jawed stupor she'd fallen into. Stepping back and opening the door wide, she said, "Sure. C'mon in."

"Thanks." He wheeled in his suitcase then set the bakery bag on top. After she'd closed and locked the door, he reached out and clasped her hands, loosely entwining their fingers. Heat prowled up her arms at the contact and she barely refrained from heaving a gushy sigh.

"I could have sent any one of my managers to handle this project," he said, his thumbs tracing slowly across the backs of her hands. "But I wanted, very much, to see you again." He released her hands then drew her into his arms. "Now, about that kiss I promised you…"

His lips brushed over hers, once, twice, a soft, teasing, searching reacquaintance that fed the fire just looking at him had kindled in her veins. She looped her arms around his neck, pressing closer until a sheet of paper couldn't have squeezed between them. Her fingers sifted through his thick, dark hair, their tongues met, and her entire body seemed to breathe out the word *finally* with a long sigh of pleasure.

That long, slow, deep, wet, "hello" kiss utterly

seduced her, ensnaring her senses, pulsing wants, needs, demands to her every nerve ending. Had she actually managed to convince herself that this spark between them wasn't pure and utter magic? Her control was evaporating at an alarming rate, punctuated by vivid mental images of her ripping off his clothing right where he stood. When he finally lifted his head, she somehow found the strength to drag open her heavy eyelids. He looked down at her with a hot, glazed expression that rushed liquid fire through her.

"Don't let go of me just yet," she requested in a breathless, husky voice. "I seem to have lost all track of my knees."

His gaze searched her face, his expression as bemused as she knew hers had to be. "I wasn't wrong."

A laugh escaped from between her lips, lifting one corner of her mouth. "I'd try to act surprised that those words would cross a man's lips, but an actress I am not. What weren't you wrong about?"

"Your kiss. Your taste." He shifted against her, shooting fiery arrows of want straight to her core. "The way you feel in my arms. I'd started to think I'd just imagined this…whatever it is you do to me, but it's just as I remembered. Even better, maybe."

The best lawyer in the world couldn't refute that statement. "But you're not *sure* it's better?" she asked. "Because I'm willing to endure another kiss if you require further proof—"

His lips captured her once again, cutting off her words, her thoughts, everything except the bewitching friction of his tongue rubbing slowly against hers, the silky heat of his mouth, the crisp, clean scent of his skin filling all the empty spaces he'd created in her head, his strong hands skimming down her back to mold her tightly against him. When what little control she'd managed to retain almost dwindled to nonexistent, she broke off their kiss.

"You have this *really* detrimental effect on my self-control," she said, her breath coming in harsh pants, "that I'm not sure I'm happy about."

"Back at ya."

"Any more proof and I'll strip you bare right here in the foyer, then drag you off to my lair to have my wicked way with you."

He groaned and leaned down to kiss the sensitive juncture where her neck and shoulder met. "And that would be bad because…why exactly?" His warm breath tickled against the skin he'd just laved with his tongue, and her eyes glazed over.

Probably there was a reason, but darned if she could think of it. How was she supposed to think of anything, with his lips marauding over her neck, and his hands cupping her breasts, his clever fingers arousing her nipples through the stretchy material of her tank top. The man was a hazard. A concentration-destroyer of the first order. She needed to do something about this—the way he made her lose her marbles just wasn't *right*.

She, too, had wondered if her imagination had overblown what they'd shared. Had it really been that good between them? Only one way to find out….

Splaying her hands against his chest, she eased back from him, then held him at arm's length. After pulling in a deep, much-needed breath, she shot him a look ripe with speculation. "Now that you mention it, I can't think of one reason why I shouldn't have my wicked way with you." She adopted her most innocent expression. "Oh—unless you'd rather watch some TV? Probably there's a tennis match on."

"You've got to be kidding."

"Some dinner? I have leftover pasta."

"Maybe later."

"Doughnut?"

"No, thanks."

"Drink?"

"You're killing me."

"I guess that's a 'no' on the drink."

"Right. About that stripping thing..." He spread his arms. "Consider me at your disposal."

9

OH MY. Riley tapped her chin with her index finger and let her gaze roam over him. Hmm. Just because she wanted to divest herself of "dull and boring" didn't mean she wanted to lose her control, as well. Here was a perfect opportunity for her to remain in control—if for no other reason than to prove to herself that she could—and in the process, to make him lose his. He was at her disposal? A very tantalizing proposition. And one that made her feel very daring indeed…

Slipping her hands under his jacket, she slowly eased the garment off his shoulders. "All you need to do is stand still."

"Stand still. I can do that."

"Let's see." She eased his jacket down his arms, then lightly tossed the dark blue pinstripe over the brass coat rack in the corner. Then she splayed her hands on his firm abdomen and walked her fingers up the front of his shirt to his tie. With her gaze steady on his, she slowly slipped the Windsor knot free, reveling in the feminine power suffusing her at the desire so evident in his eyes.

She slipped the ends of his shirt from his waist-band, then slowly unbuttoned the snowy cotton. She guided the material off his broad shoulders, then down his arms. Before she hung the shirt on the coat rack, she buried her face in the soft cotton, still warm from his skin and breathed deeply.

"Hmm," she said. "Fresh laundry and warm man. Very nice."

She rested her palms on his shoulders, then spread her fingers and slowly dragged her hands downward. His muscles jumped beneath her fingers, and she noted that he clenched his hands at his sides. "Problem?" she whispered.

"No. But I don't know how long I'll be able to stand still when my control is already sorely tested three seconds in."

She fought to suppress the satisfied smile that pulled at her lips, not to mention the relief that it wasn't just her experiencing control problems here. She trailed her fingertips lightly over him, skimming over those lovely washboard abs, then stepped closer to place an openmouthed kiss in the center of his chest. After dragging her tongue across his hair-roughened skin, she sought out his nipple, drawing its velvety smoothness into her mouth. A low growl vibrated in his throat and, encouraged by his response, she kissed her way across his chest to lave his other nipple, reveling in the gentle scrape of his silky, coarse chest hair against her cheek. She drew a deep breath, filling her head with his crisp, clean scent. Her tongue flicked over his nipple again, and he sifted his fingers through her hair.

She immediately pulled back and with a mock frown, shook her finger at him. "That's not standing still."

Arousal darkened his eyes, and he slowly lowered his hands to his sides. "I can see that this is going to prove a true test of my self-control."

"That's the plan. How is your self-control, by the way?"

"Normally? Formidable. Right now? I'm definitely detecting a few dents in the armor."

"How...intriguing. Let's see just how many dents I can find." She slowly ran her fingers up and down his chest, relearning each fascinating slope of muscle, enjoying his low moans of pleasure. When she ran a single fingertip around his skin just above the waistband of his trousers, a visible shudder ran through him. Delighted, she gently tapped one of his black-tasseled Loafers with her bare toes. "Shoes and socks off."

He toed off his shoes, stripped off his socks, then stood before her, the heat emanating from him along with the sensual gleam in his eye leaving her in no doubt that he was looking forward to whatever she had planned.

"You look really great wearing nothing but those pants," she said, her appreciative gaze tracking over him while her fingertip drew lazy circles around his navel.

"Thanks," he said in a tight voice.

She unbuckled his belt then flicked open the button on his pants. "But you look even greater wearing...nothing."

A muscle jumped in his jaw while she slowly lowered his zipper. Then, sliding her hands under the waistband of his boxers, she lowered his pants and underwear in a single smooth motion. He stepped out of the clothes and shoved them aside with his foot.

"Oh, my," she said, her gaze riveted on his erection. She reached out a single fingertip and circled the engorged head with a feathery touch that had him sucking in a sharp breath. "You know," she said in a deliberately smoky purr, "clothes may make the

man, but it's the naked man that gets my attention."
Her leisurely circling continued, and she watched his
muscles bunch in his obvious fight to maintain control. Her other hand joined in the act, reaching behind him to tickle lightly over his buttocks.

"Spread your legs," she whispered, skimming her
hand down his thigh.

Once he'd widened his stance, she shot him a
wicked grin. "Hands above your head."

He cocked a brow. "Is this a stickup?"

Her gaze flicked down to his rigid penis. "Hmm.
So it would seem."

With his heated gaze burning into hers, he raised
his arms and rested his clasped hands on top of his
head. "Am I under arrest?"

"Depends on whether or not I find any concealed
weapons during my search."

"I'd have a hard time concealing anything like
this."

"A hard time," she repeated slowly, her fingers
dipping into the crease of his thighs to cup him. "Yes,
I can see that."

Flattening her palm just below his navel, she
walked behind him, dragging her hand across his
hip. When she stood directly behind him, she allowed her avid gaze to roam over him.

"Very nice view," she said, resting her hands on
the back of his thighs, then trailing her fingers slowly
upward, over his firm buttocks, then higher, until
she reached his shoulders.

"Glad you like it—"

His words ended in a groan as she stepped up behind him and pressed herself against his back.
Reaching her arms around him, she allowed her fingers to map a leisurely path along the fascinating

contours of his body, absorbing every shudder and moan he made. She took her time, her lips exploring his smooth back while her fingers danced over his front, touching him everywhere—except his arousal.

"You're doing a great job of standing still," she whispered against his neck.

"It's costing me, believe me," he said, his voice jagged with want.

"Very impressive control." She wrapped one hand around his erection and squeezed, while her other hand reached lower to lightly stroke between his legs.

A feral groan escaped him and he dipped his chin. Knowing he was watching her hands, Riley caressed his hard, silky flesh, stroking the length of him, circling him, cupping, teasing, relentlessly arousing him, her own arousal increasing in tandem.

"I'm not going to last much longer." His words ended on a gravelly groan and she could see, feel, his muscles straining to keep himself in check. She squeezed his arousal and with a guttural moan he strained forward and thrust into her hand.

She released him, then moved around until she faced him. The heat burning in his eyes scorched her. Without a word, she gently pushed him backward until his shoulders met the wall. Then she sunk to her knees in front of him and slowly drew him into her mouth.

Jackson's head dropped back against the wall and he sucked in a sharp breath as her warm mouth closed over him. He released that breath in a long hiss of pleasure as her tongue slowly circled him, tormenting, teasing, driving him crazy. Lifting his head, he looked down and watched her slowly draw him more deeply into the heated velvet of her mouth.

Her hands were relentless, dipping between his legs to cup him, skimming over his thighs, grasping the base of his shaft.

He gritted his teeth and fought against the rapidly approaching need to come until he knew the battle was about to be lost. Unclasping his hands, he grabbed her shoulders and pulled her to her feet. Then he dipped his knees and swung her up into his arms.

"Armor's dented and gone," he announced in a gravelly voice he'd never heard before. "Where's your bedroom?"

She wrapped her arms around his neck and pointed toward a hallway on the right with her chin. "Second door on the left."

He moved swiftly in the direction she'd indicated. "You have condoms?" he managed to ask, praying she did so he wouldn't have to stop and go digging through his suitcase to find his supply.

She nodded. "In the bedside table."

When they reached her bedroom, he set her on her feet near the edge of the bed. When she reached for him, he lightly clasped her wrists and shook his head. "My turn. All you need to do is stand still."

Her golden brown eyes looked like glittering topazes and her throat moved as she swallowed.

"Hands above your head," he said, lifting her arms. Just as he'd done, she clasped her hands on top of her head. "Is this a stickup?" she asked, repeating his earlier words in a throaty voice.

"Search and seizure." He slipped his hands beneath her stretchy turquoise tank top, skating over her warm, trim stomach, smoothing his palms up her rib cage. Her breasts filled his palms and he watched her eyes drift closed as his fingers grazed over her aroused nipples. He slid the soft material up, over her arms, then tossed the shirt on the bed. He lightly circled the soft fullness of her breasts before dipping his head to draw first one pebbled nipple, then the other into his mouth.

He kissed his way back up to her neck to absorb with his lips the long purr of pleasure vibrating from her throat, while his fingers undid the button on her denim shorts, then lowered the zipper. After slipping his hands inside, he cupped the bare curve of her buttocks and groaned. Or was that her?

His arousal strained, and he had to grit his teeth to fight off the urge to simply devour her. Forcing himself to take his time, he slowly dragged her shorts and panties down her legs. When they fell to her ankles, she stepped out of the discarded items.

Jackson took a single step backward and for several seconds just looked at her, naked, gorgeous, flushed and aroused, lips parted, eyes smoky, her uplifted arms jutting her breasts forward. Reaching out, he grasped her waist, turned her around, then stepped up close behind her. With his erection nestled between her buttocks, his mouth feasted on her delicate, vanilla-scented nape. He cupped her breasts, kneading their fullness, teasing her hard nipples. Her head fell back against his shoulder and she pressed back against him, slowly gyrating her hips. His erection jerked against her buttocks and a low growl rumbled in his throat.

"That's not standing still," he grated against her neck.

"So sue me," she said, the words ending on a moan as one of his hands skimmed down her belly to tangle in the curls at the apex of her thighs.

"Spread your legs, Riley," he whispered against her ear.

She did as he said, and his fingers slipped between her thighs to caress her wet, swollen folds. He breathed deeply, filling his head with her delicious vanilla scent mixed with the erotic musk of female arousal.

"That's not going to help me stand still," she said, grinding back against him. "Neither is that," she added with a groan when he slipped two fingers inside her velvet heat.

Slowly stroking her, he whispered against her neck, "The fact that you can't remain still…I don't know if that means you're really good at this game, or really bad at it."

"Hmm. Don't know. Don't care. I'm…ooh, more than willing to concede victory to you."

He slipped his fingers from her, and she made a sound of protest—a sound that morphed into a prolonged, voluptuous sigh when he scooped her up, laid her on the bed, then kneeled between her splayed thighs.

She reached out, slid open the bedside table drawer, and withdrew a foil packet, which she tossed lightly on the bedspread within easy reach. With her glittering gaze locked on his, she said, "Ready when you are."

"Good to know. But not just yet…"

After gliding his hands up her silky smooth legs, he gently pressed against her inner thighs, spreading her legs wider. She bent her knees and for several pounding heartbeats he just looked at her, softly illuminated by the light spilling in from the hallway. Her dark hair was tousled, shiny curls spread around her head like a halo, but that was the only thing angelic about the way she looked. With her arms raised above her head, eyelids at half-mast, nipples erect from his mouth and hands, legs parted to reveal her glistening sex, she looked like living, breathing sin.

He leaned over her and pressed his lips to the delicate indentation at the base of her throat, then traced a line down her body with his tongue. Cupping her buttocks in his palms, he lifted her, making love to her with his mouth, tasting, caressing, teasing her swollen feminine folds until she arched her back and cried out her release. Then he reached for the condom, quickly sheathed himself, and slid deep into her tight heat.

Propping his weight on his forearms, he looked down into her flushed face. "Look at me," he rasped.

Golden brown eyes, blurry with arousal, flickered open. When they focused on him, he and Riley simply looked at each other for several seconds. She reached up, tunneled her fingers in his hair, and with a sound that resembled a growl, dragged his head down for a deep, lush kiss. He stroked inside her slowly, withdrawing nearly all the way before sliding deep again, gritting his teeth against the intense pleasure, trying to retain the last bit of his control against the increasingly desperate need to come. When she wrapped her arms and legs around him, urging him faster, deeper, then arched her back and tightened around him, the battle was lost. His release thundered through him, ripping a jagged moan from his throat. When his shudders subsided, he rested his damp forehead against hers, their ragged breaths mingling.

He was still fighting for breath when she spoke. "Okay," she whispered. "This little episode has proven beyond any doubt that you simply have the most disruptive effect on my control. It's like one touch, and *poof!* I'm a goner."

Jackson somehow found the strength to lift his head. Masculine satisfaction rushed through him at her flushed cheeks and bemused expression. "You say that like it's a bad thing."

"I think it might be. I *like* being in control."

"You can be on top anytime you want."

She narrowed her eyes. "That's not what I mean."

"I know." He brushed a tangled curl from her cheek, then glided the pad of his thumb over her smooth cheek. "And I know exactly what you mean because my reaction to you...it borders on the ridiculous. Believe it or not, I didn't come here tonight thinking we'd be naked within three minutes."

She raised her brows. "Oh? How long had you planned it would take? Five minutes?"

He laughed and pressed a kiss to the tip of her nose. "More like ten. Hopefully less than fifteen. I don't think I would have made it more than twenty." He ran the tip of his tongue over her plump lower lip. "I was wanting you in a *very* serious way."

"Really?" She tickled her fingers down his spine to his buttocks, mischief dancing in her eyes. "I hadn't particularly noticed."

"Then we'll just have to try it again so you can pay attention next time."

"A harsh punishment, but I'll try my best to live with it."

"Before next time happens, I'm going to need some refueling. Did I hear an offer of pasta earlier?"

"You did. You certainly picked a good night to drop by—last night was just tuna salad. I'll have a doughnut while you're eating. Madame Sees-All predicts we're going to need those carbs before morning."

He raised his brows. "Is that an invitation to spend the night?"

"Yeah, I guess it is. Tara's sleeping at a friend's apartment, so I have the place to myself. Wanna stay over for a slumber party?"

"That depends—does 'slumber' actually need to be involved?"

She laughed. "At some point, probably. So we don't doze off in meetings tomorrow. I'm going to make it my night's goal to tire you out."

He looked down into her glowing, smiling eyes and realized this was the happiest he'd felt in a very long time. Man, nothing like great sex and the promise of a meal to pile on the contentment. But the moment the thought entered his head, everything inside him said, *This spark feels like a helluva lot more than sex and pasta.*

Whatever it was, he intended to enjoy it while it lasted.

Smiling down at her, he said, "Bring it on, Sweet Stuff."

THE INSTANT Riley and Gloria sat down to lunch at a table tucked away in the corner of the office building café the next afternoon, Gloria said, "Okay, tell me everything."

Riley drizzled some low-fat dressing on her salad, a concession made necessary by the doughnuts she'd eaten last night. "You first," she said. "How was the conference?"

"Fun. Tiring. Normal conference stuff. I'm much more interested in why you're absolutely glowing when *I'm* the one who plopped down the big bucks for a facial." Gloria squinted at her from across the table. "Either you swallowed a neon bulb, or you've recently had some fabulous sex."

Riley stabbed a cucumber with her fork and waggled her brows. "Jackson's in town on business. He spent the night last night."

Gloria dropped her plastic fork and leaned forward. "You didn't tell me he was coming back!"

"I didn't know. He just showed up at my apartment, bearing doughnuts."

"Ooh, doughnuts. No wonder you invited him to spend the night," Gloria said with a smile.

"Right. Because I wouldn't have otherwise."

"So you had a fabulous night…?"

Riley nodded. "Very fabulous. I'm thinking that maybe he's not as annoying as I'd originally thought."

Gloria laughed. "Honey, you've been thinking that since Marcus's picnic."

Had she? Riley's brows pulled down and she thoughtfully chewed a carrot slice. She mentally ran through a list of words she'd now use to describe Jackson—funny, intelligent, honest, hardworking, likeable, generous, sexy, handsome. Nope, annoying was no longer on the list. When exactly had that happened?

"It would seem that somewhere between making love with him, sharing phone calls and e-mails, and that late-night budget go-round at the office, my opinion of him has changed." Spearing a cherry tomato, she said slowly, "Gloria, I think I…*like* him."

"And you make this sound like bad news because…?"

"For starters, he lives in New York."

"Not if the merger goes through and his job relocates to Atlanta."

"Just because his job would relocate doesn't mean *he* would."

"If he makes this merger happen, you know they'll make him a fabulous offer."

"True…but then there's the fact that Jackson and I have so little in common." Yet even as she said the words, Riley had to question exactly how valid they were. "Although," she added slowly, "as I've discovered through our conversations and e-mails, it isn't as if we have *nothing* in common." She shook her head. "But you and I both know that opposites don't really attract. Not for the long haul."

"To which I have two things to say," Gloria replied, ticking the items off on her manicured fingers. "One, who says you have to be in this for the long haul? And two, maybe these things you don't have in common could actually prove…interesting. Just because baseball isn't his favorite sport doesn't mean he couldn't enjoy it, especially if you put a little effort into it."

"Like what? Sit on his lap and feed him salted peanuts?"

Gloria nodded enthusiastically. "Excellent idea."

"I was *joking*."

"I wasn't. That would certainly increase his interest quotient more than firing off a bunch of batting stats. And you don't have to be in love with art museums to spend an afternoon at one. If the paintings start to bore you, you could always check out—"

"—Jackson's great…assets?"

"Exactly."

"In other words, sometimes it's not where you go, it's who you go there with."

"*Now* you're thinking outside the box," Gloria said with an approving nod. A wicked grin pulled up her lips. "Throw in some sexy lingerie and you'll put a whole new spin on a day at the museum. When are you seeing him again?"

"Tonight. He was scheduled to fly to New York tomorrow evening, then come back to Atlanta Monday morning, but I invited him to spend the weekend with me." A tingle zoomed through her just saying it out loud.

"An entire weekend together," Gloria said, nodding. "Excellent. By Sunday night, you'll have a good idea what he's really like, and if you do indeed really like him. Do you have anything special planned?"

"No. Tara is leaving on Saturday, so most of the day will be spent moving out her stuff and loading the U-Haul she rented." Riley shook her head and laughed. "I can't believe how much she has."

"Jackson knows this is happening Saturday?"

"Yes. He offered to help."

Gloria stared. "He *offered* to lift and lug and cart and crate a bunch of heavy boxes and furniture all day on his day off? Be still my heart. Tell me—what's the brother situation with him?"

"Has two, but one's getting married soon and the other's too young."

"How young? If he's close to legal age, we've got something to work with."

Riley laughed. "He's more Tara's cup of tea."

"Damn. Frat-boy type, huh?"

"'Fraid so. Besides, what do you need with another man? I thought things were going great with you and Rob."

A shade of pink Riley had never witnessed on Gloria's skin colored her friend's cheeks. "Actually, things are going *really* great with Rob. And I'll tell you all about it after we're done talking about Jackson." Gloria's expression turned serious. "You seem to know a lot about his family."

"We've spent a lot of time on the phone."

"And you've liked what you've heard?"

Riley drew a deep breath, her mind replaying snippets of conversations she'd shared with Jackson. Finally, she said, "Yes."

"You don't sound particularly happy about that."

"I'm not sure I am." She lifted her gaze from her half-eaten salad and voiced the worry that had been darting around in her brain for longer than she cared to admit. "I'm afraid I might be developing some...*feelings* for Jackson."

"And that scares you."

It wasn't a question, but Riley nodded. "Yes. It's caught me off guard. You know how I like to plan things."

"I do. But feelings, unfortunately, rarely cooperate with plans."

"Tell me about it. After Tara moved out, the plan was to make up for lost time as a freewheeling bachelorette. Have fun. Date a slew of different men."

Gloria patted her hand in sympathy. "And now you only want to date one particular man."

"Seems so. Which really messes up the whole freewheeling bachelorette plan. I hadn't anticipated jumping right into a long-term relationship."

"True, but don't do that 'can't see the forest for the trees' routine, Riley. Maybe, just maybe, Jackson is *the* guy." Gloria glanced at her watch. "Listen, I'm sorry to cut our lunch short, but I have a meeting scheduled in five minutes. Call me if you need to talk. And think about what I said."

Riley nodded, then took a long drink of her water, Gloria's words reverberating in her mind. *Maybe Jackson is the guy.*

Think about what she said? A humorless laugh escaped Riley. She didn't think she'd be able to think about anything else.

10

JUST BEFORE noon on Saturday, Riley opened her refrigerator and breathed a sigh of relief at the blast of cold air that hit her. She attempted to blow off the lank strands of hair sticking to her forehead, but no luck. With the temperature hovering right around the one-hundred-degree mark, hot, sticky and sweaty was about the best anyone could expect. Just as she pulled out the pitcher of iced tea, Tara re-entered the apartment.

"Jackson is loading the last of the boxes into the U-Haul," Tara said, her voice filled with relief. Sweat beaded on her flushed cheeks as she opened the cabinet to take out three tea glasses. "He's been a godsend, Riley. Not only can he lift and haul, he packs a car like a pro and looks damn good doing it."

"Yes, he does," Riley agreed, enjoying the blast of icy air when she opened the freezer to get the ice cubes. "I don't need a mirror to know that I look like something a dog would be tempted to bury in the backyard, while he looks rumpled and yummy the way only a sweaty, rumpled man can."

"It's totally unfair," Tara grumbled while filling the glasses with ice.

"It certainly is. Women not only have to deal with mascara, panty hose and high heels, we also get stuck looking sweaty and disheveled as soon as the mercury rises a few degrees. Who made up those rules?"

"Some man. But we live in Atlanta, and as you know, women here don't sweat, we—"

"*Glisten*," they said together, then laughed.

After Riley filled the three glasses and her sister added festive lemon slices, she lifted a glass and smiled at her younger sibling. "Here's to a safe journey."

Tara tapped her glass rim to Riley's, and they both drank deeply. Riley set her glass on the counter and grabbed the third glass. "I'm going to bring this out to Jackson."

Tara stopped her, laying her hand on Riley's arm. "Can I talk to you for a second first?"

Riley set the glass back down. "Sure. What's up?"

Tara looked at the floor and tucked a loose strand of shiny brown hair behind her ear. It suddenly struck Riley how young and innocent her sister looked. With her extraordinarily pretty face scrubbed free of makeup, and her hair clipped back in a haphazard ponytail, Tara looked sweet and much too young to be venturing out on her own.

When Tara looked up, Riley noted the seriousness reflected in her hazel eyes. "I just wanted to tell you that I really appreciate your putting up with me these past five years, Riley."

A rush of emotion swelled Riley's throat. "I know, Tara."

"I'm not sure how you *could*, because I know I didn't tell you nearly often enough." She reached out and clasped Riley's hands. "But I do appreciate it. If it weren't for you, I wouldn't have finished college. I guess I just want to thank you for all the times you were hard on me and didn't let me get away with stuff and forced me to take responsibility for my actions. I may not have liked it at the time, but looking back…well, I'm grateful. I know I haven't been the easiest person to live with, and that you sacrificed a lot, but you never bailed on me or gave up on me."

"You weren't *that* bad," Riley said, hoping her smile appeared less wobbly than it felt. "Usually."

"I know I caused you plenty of headaches. I also wanted to thank you for all the times you encouraged me and rescued me and helped me with my accounting homework." She squeezed Riley's hands and gave her a shaky smile, her hazel eyes huge and glossy with unshed tears. "I love you, Riley."

"I love you, too, sweetie," Riley said, her own eyes filling with tears. She pulled Tara close and they shared a hug. "And I'm really proud of you."

"Thanks." They pulled apart, then laughed at themselves, both reaching for paper towels to dab at their wet eyes. "Jackson's great," Tara said, after she'd dried her eyes.

Riley smiled. "He's not too bad."

"Not too bad?" Tara laughed. "You've always been the queen of the understatement. He's totally hot, Riley. And he's totally nuts about you."

"I know he *likes* me, but—"

"He more than likes you."

Riley stilled. "What makes you say that?"

Tara looked at the ceiling and although she didn't say *duh*, she might as well have. "The way he looks at you, the way he smiles at you, the way he talks to you. Everything. Trust me on this—the guy is head over heels."

Riley wasn't quite sure how to—or if she even wanted to—tell Tara that Jackson's state of being head over heels was nothing more than a guy in the throws of sexual attraction. Before she could decide what to say, Tara added, "And based on the way you look at him, it's clear the feeling's mutual."

"Obviously I like him—"

"Uh-huh. Like. Sort of a lukewarm word for the fireworks I sense exploding between you two."

Riley's brows drew together. Tara was right. *Like* didn't begin to describe the maelstrom of Jackson-inspired feelings swirling through her. But if it wasn't like, then it must be...

Oh, boy.

Had she actually fallen in love? That didn't bode well for her plans for a bachelorette, reclaim-her-youth lifestyle.

She felt a hand on her arm and noticed Tara looking at her with concern. "Are you all right, Riley?"

An unsteady laugh escaped her. "I'm not sure."

Tara studied her for several seconds, then said, "You're falling for him."

"When did you get so perceptive?"

"Always have been." She grinned. "It's why my friends call me at all hours of the night to talk. They call me the Relationship Doctor."

"You're kidding."

"I'm not. Want my advice?"

"No. Yes. I don't know." She rammed her hands into her pockets. "I'm not even sure how this happened. A month ago, I couldn't stand this man."

"If I recall correctly the little bit you've told me, you hadn't even met him in person until three weeks ago. You didn't know him. Hadn't spent any time with him. It's pretty obvious that now you can stand him."

"I can. What I can't stand is the thought of being

away from him. And that scares me. This was supposed to be nothing more than a bit of fun. It's happening too fast, but it's like a snowball rolling downhill—I can't stop the momentum. I tell myself that I don't know him very well, that we live in different cities, that we have different interests, but none of that seems to matter. Then I tell myself that I'm learning more about him every day, his job will most likely relocate to Atlanta, and even though we're different, we seem to agree on the important stuff. But throwing my heart into the ring—that's scary."

"You know, Mom and Dad fell in love quick."

A sad smile pulled at Riley's lips. "Yes, they did. So you think it's in the gene pool?"

"Yeah, I do," Tara said, her voice serious. "You've always been a great judge of character, Riley. Listen to what your heart tells you."

Riley drew in a slow, deep breath. She wasn't quite ready to examine her heart too closely. She wanted, needed more time. Falling in love quickly was one thing—warp speed was quite another.

"As for throwing your heart in the ring," Tara said, "remember this—if you want to reach the next branch, you have to go out on a limb."

Riley smiled, then shook her head, bemused. "*How* did you become so wise about matters of the heart?"

"Practice." An impish grin curved her lips. "What do you think I was doing all those hours I was supposed to be studying?"

Riley groaned. "I don't want to hear it."

"Just think about what I said."

She was saved from replying when the front door opened then closed.

"Car and U-Haul are all packed," came Jackson's deep voice. Seconds later, he appeared in the archway leading to the kitchen and wiped his sweaty forehead with an equally sweaty forearm. Riley handed him a glass of iced tea, which he accepted with a grateful smile. He brought the glass to his lips and she watched him down the entire contents, her gaze wandering over him. How he managed to look so delicious wearing an old gray T-shirt sporting the name of a New York gym, navy blue shorts bearing the same logo, and sneakers that looked as if he'd trekked across country with them was a mystery, but there you had it. Undeniable. Just like her growing feelings for him—feelings that involved a whole lot more than just sex. Since she didn't know just what she planned to do about that, she filed the problem away, to be audited at a later date.

After he'd drained the glass, he exhaled a satisfied *aah*, then smiled. "Thanks. I needed that." His gaze bounced between her and Tara, then a wary look entered his eyes. "Everything okay here?"

"Fine," Riley said.

"You sure?" He made sniffing noises. "I smell tears. *Girl* tears."

"Maybe a few." She couldn't help but laugh at the cautious backward step he took. "Oh, c'mon. A big, strapping guy like you can't be afraid of a few little tears."

"The hell I can't." He backed up another step. "I'd rather face a pack of starving wolves with a pork chop hung around my neck. I'll just leave you two ladies to finish up your sisterly stuff."

"We're finished," Tara assured him with a smile. She picked up her keys from the counter and twirled them around on her index finger. "I'm ready to go."

Riley and Jackson escorted Tara to her car. "Don't forget to call so I know you arrived safely," Riley said. "And please drive carefully."

"Yes, ma'am," Tara said with a teasing grin. She turned to Jackson and, after giving him a hug and a resounding kiss on the cheek, said, "It was great meeting you. I really appreciate all the help today. If you ever decide to go into the moving business, I'll write you a glowing reference."

Jackson smiled. "Thanks. Good luck with your new apartment and job."

Tara then turned to Riley and hugged her tightly. "Hold on to this guy. He's a keeper," Tara whispered. "You'll have to tell me later if he has a brother. Love you, sis."

"Love you, too," Riley whispered back around the lump that was swelling her throat at an alarming rate.

Tara climbed into her car, started the engine, then, with a cheery smile and wave out the window, drove toward the exit. Riley continued to stare at the corner even after Tara's car had turned and disappeared from view, until Jackson cleared his throat, regaining her attention.

"You okay?" he asked, touching her arm.

To Riley's dismay, her bottom lip trembled and hot tears pushed behind her eyeballs. She blinked rapidly and nodded...then shook her head as a big tear dribbled down her cheek.

"Aw, Riley. Come here, sweetheart." He opened his arms and Riley stepped into his embrace and wrapped her arms around his waist. Burying her face against his chest, she let loose the sobs she couldn't contain while he patted her back, pressed soft kisses against her hair and whispered calming words against her ear.

Finally she lifted her wet face. "I don't know what's wrong with me," she said, shaking her head, tears still leaking from her eyes. "I thought I'd be happy to see her go, but look at me—I'm a mess."

He brushed away her tears with gentle strokes of his thumbs while his gaze roamed her face. "Not a mess. Just a little...tear-stained."

"I meant in here." She patted her hand against her chest. "Half of me is so happy she's gone, half of me is so guilty for feeling that way, and the other half already misses her."

A lopsided smile tilted Jackson's lips. "Obviously you're upset because that's *three* halves. If your numbers aren't adding up, you need help." He dropped a kiss on the tip of her nose. "I understand how you're feeling. When Brian moved out of my place, I thought I'd break into the 'Hallelujah Chorus'— which part of me did, believe me. But there was this other part that suddenly understood what my folks must have felt when we all left the nest."

Riley nodded. "That's it. I'm suffering from empty-nest syndrome, and I'm not even a mom yet."

"Look at it as good practice for the future." His gaze suddenly turned thoughtful. "You did a good job with your sister, Riley. You're understanding, responsible and patient. Kind and loving. You'll make a good mom someday."

Something in his voice, in the sudden seriousness reflected in his eyes, hitched her breath. Before she could even think of a reply, a musical beep sounded. He immediately tensed, then reached into his back pocket. "That's my phone."

"Is it the call you've been waiting for?" He'd told her all about his sister, her pregnancy and today's sonogram.

"It's Shelley," he confirmed after looking at the caller ID display.

Riley motioned that she'd wait inside, but he snagged her hand and shook his head. "Stay with me." Then he said into the phone, "Hi, Shell. How are you, kiddo?"

Riley watched his brows draw together, sensed the taut set of his shoulders, felt his tension in the way he gripped her hand. She pressed her lips together, praying his sister's news would be good. He squeezed his eyes shut, then blew out a long breath. When he opened his eyes, his wide grin could have lit a dark room.

"That's great news, Shell." He shifted the phone away from his mouth and whispered, "She's fine. Baby's perfect." Riley released a breath she hadn't even realized she held and shot him a thumbs-up with her free hand. He then said into the phone, "Do we know if it's a boy or a girl?" He listened for several seconds, then his grin widened. Again he moved the phone from his mouth and whispered to Riley, "We're having a girl." He returned his attention to the phone, and Riley watched him listen to whatever his sister said. He nodded a few times, then laughed and said, "You go get 'em tiger. Can't wait to see you and give ya a big hug. And get the kid's nursery ready. I'll be bringing home a boatload of pink stuff from Atlanta." His gaze shifted to Riley as he listened, then he said softly, "Yeah, Atlanta's really…great. Okay. Tell everybody I say hi. I'll call next week. Love you, too. Bye."

He flipped his phone shut, slipped it into his pocket, then lifted Riley off her feet and spun her around, planting an enthusiastic kiss on her lips. "How's *that* for good news?" He set her back on her feet, but kept his arms around her and grinned.

"It's terrific," Riley said, returning his infectious smile. "I'm very happy for all of you...Uncle Jackson."

"Isn't that something? I'm gonna have a *niece*. Hey, where's the best place to shop around here? I want to buy lots of pink baby stuff."

Riley couldn't help but laugh. "You're the first man I've ever heard ask to go shopping, and for pink stuff, no less."

He dipped his knees, and before she could catch her breath, he'd swung her up into his arms and headed toward her apartment. "Between you successfully sending Tara off and Shelley's baby news, this has been a banner day."

"I agree. Let's celebrate."

"Excellent idea. And I know just what we should do."

"What's that?"

"Let's get naked and I'll show you."

Heat curled down to her toes. "Actually, I already have a surprise planned for this evening. It will be the perfect way to celebrate."

"Does it involve getting naked?" He nuzzled her neck, his teeth lightly abrading her skin, skittering tingles down Riley's spine. "'Cause I really, really want to get naked with you."

Seeing as how she really, really wanted to get naked with him, too, she didn't argue. "How about we get naked and take a shower together?"

"A great way to save water. Have I mentioned that I admire your frugal nature?"

"Actually, no." She rifled her fingers through the hair at his nape and stretched her neck to afford his lips easier access to her throat. "In fact, as I recall, it tends to annoy you."

"I've changed my mind. It's now near the top of my *Things I Like About You* list." They reached her apartment. Instead of putting her down, he simply bent his knees and opened the door, which Riley shoved closed with her foot after they'd entered the foyer.

"You have a list?" she asked, her arms clinging around his neck as he locked the door, then headed purposefully toward the bathroom.

"Yeah. You know what's in the number one spot right now?"

"The fact that I'm about to get naked and soapy with you?"

"You know, I think you may really be clairvoyant, Madame Sees-All. If being an accountant doesn't work out, you might want to give fortune-telling a try for real."

She leaned forward to bite his earlobe lightly, and was rewarded with a low growl. "Wait till you hear what I predict for the next thirty minutes of your future."

"Bring it on, Sweet Stuff."

AT EIGHT O'CLOCK THAT EVENING, Jackson craned his neck to take a good look around him, then shook his head, still not certain how this had all come about. Leaning closer to Riley, he said in an undertone, "When you said we'd celebrate, I was sort of thinking champagne and sex. Not baseball."

She shot him a slow, seductive smile that somehow managed to make him forget the noise of the thousands of Braves fans surrounding them. "Now who's thinking inside the box?" she asked. "Besides, we had sex. In the shower, remember?"

He screwed up his face, then shook his head. "I'm having a lapse here. My memory needs refreshing."

She tickled her fingertips over his thigh and leaned toward him to whisper, "I'll gladly refresh you the minute we get back to my place, which Madame Sees-All predicts you'll especially enjoy since I'm always keyed up after a game."

"Hmm. You're one fine fortune-teller. Maybe baseball isn't so boring after all."

"When's the last time you attended a ball game?"

"You mean before this?"

"Yes."

"Never."

She leaned back and stared at him. "You live in New York and you've never been to Yankee Stadium?"

"Nope."

"Shea Stadium?"

"Never. Now, if you want to talk about Madison Square Garden and basketball, or Flushing Meadow and tennis, I'm your guy."

"Wow. Well, you have a lot to learn, and I'm just the gal to teach you what you've been missing. The first of which is snacks." She dragged a tortilla chip through some spicy melted cheese, then held the treat out to him. He ate the chip, but sort of forgot how to chew when she slipped her finger into her mouth to suck off a bit of cheese.

He managed to swallow without choking, then shifted in his seat. "If you keep doing that, I won't make it nine innings."

Devilry danced in her eyes. "Oh, dear. If you can't handle the nachos, you're going to have a real problem at the seventh inning stretch."

"What happens then?"

"Everybody stands up and sings 'Take Me Out to the Ball Game.'"

"I'm not much of a singer, but I think I can handle that."

"Then I hit the concession stand and buy my favorite late innings treat—a cherry Popsicle."

An image of her sucking on a Popsicle flashed in his mind and he groaned. "Not sure I can handle that."

"Then I'd better not tell you the extra treat I have planned for you if the Braves actually win this game."

"I can handle it. Tell me."

She pressed her lips against his ear and whispered. He knew his eyes had glazed over before she even reached the good part. When she finished, she leaned back, raised her brows and smiled. "What do you have to say to that, Tennis-Man?"

It sure as hell wasn't easy to think, what with all his blood cells now settled in his groin, but Jackson pulled in a deep breath, whistled through his teeth, then pumped his fist in the air. "Go, Braves!"

JACKSON AWOKE TO THE WARMTH of sunshine seeping through the blinds, the cheery chirping of birds outside the window, and the tantalizing aroma of sizzling bacon and fresh-brewed coffee. After rolling over onto his back, he stacked his hands beneath his head, then turned to look at the empty space where, for the past eleven nights, Riley's warm, curvy body had lain next to his. Under his. Over his.

But today was Sunday, and his flight to New York would depart at eight this evening. His project in Atlanta had been completed successfully, he'd stayed on for the weekend, but now it was time to go home.

He stared at the ceiling, a series of images from the past eleven days clicking through his mind like a PowerPoint presentation. Waking each morning to the sight and feel of Riley snuggled close to him in her bed. Morning laughs and kisses. Surprising her in the shower. Her surprising him back. Sharing coffee while getting ready for work. Then enduring hectic days filled with meetings and thoughts of her. Waiting impatiently until they could be together again in the evening. Enjoying dinners out. Dinners in. A trip to Atlanta's High Museum of Art, which Riley had grudgingly admitted she'd enjoyed. She'd shown him how much fun a baseball game on TV could be when she sat on his lap and fed him peanuts. He'd shown her how much fun a visit to the history museum could be when he discovered that Fridays were martini nights at the Fernbank Museum. Laughing, talking, learning about each other—both in and out of bed. Hours spent in sensual exploration that had done nothing to lessen the spark between them. If anything, the flame burned hotter with each new thing he discovered about her, a fact that confused him. Why hadn't it fizzled yet? How long before it did? It hadn't occurred to him that he'd spend all this time with her. Hadn't crossed his mind that he wouldn't check into a hotel. That he wouldn't want his own space. That he'd so much enjoy the intimacy of sharing her apartment all this time.

While they hadn't talked much about the future of their relationship, Jackson knew it was something they would soon need to discuss. Based on conversations he'd had during the week with Elite's CEO, it looked as if the merger with Prestige was going to take place. And although he hadn't yet heard back from Winthrop Hotels regarding his interview—which had gone very well—he expected to soon. Would they offer him the executive position?

He still debated talking to Riley about the possible Winthrop job, but decided each time to hold off. He'd told her up front that a move to Atlanta wasn't a done deal for him. His career had been and needed to continue to be his first priority. In the cutthroat world of marketing, especially in a town like New York, he couldn't afford to relax his guard.

And the unvarnished truth was that he feared if he talked to Riley about the potential Winthrop job, she might influence him in a way that he'd later regret. Better that he stood at the crossroads alone—if, indeed, it came to that and he was offered the position. They could always just enjoy the long-distance relationship they had now. Nothing wrong with that. Hell, it would make every time they saw each other feel like the first time, right? She'd already accepted his invitation to come to New York for the long holiday weekend coming up next month, and he'd told her he'd make time to come back to Atlanta after that. So far, so good. No reason to rock the boat.

A slight movement from the doorway caught his attention, and he turned his head. Riley lounged against the doorjamb, wearing the black T-shirt he'd bought her at the art museum, and a wicked smile.

"You seem lost in thought," she said in a throaty voice. "Thinking about breakfast?"

"Yeah. And the woman cooking it." His gaze wandered over her T-shirt and bare legs. "But I was picturing you naked."

"I once heard on a cooking show that it's not a good idea to cook bacon in the nude. I decided to take the chef's advice. But, that's easily remedied." She grabbed the ends of the T-shirt and in one fluid motion pulled the material over her head and sent it sailing into the corner.

Jackson's gaze leisurely strolled over all her luscious curves and he stirred against the cotton sheets.

"Breakfast is ready," she said. "But I put it in the oven to stay warm…just in case."

"Just in case of what?" he said, his attempt at feigned disinterest completely ruined by the very noticeable tenting of the sheet.

"Just in case something comes…up."

Riley looked at him, sprawled in her bed, his eyes dark with heat and desire, and an answering want shot through her. With every new experience, each new shared day, every conversation, each sensual exploration, she stepped closer and closer to the emotional abyss yawning before her. Since she was helpless to stop it, she could only hang on and hope for the best.

She lifted her arms and sifted her fingers through her tousled hair, then slowly ran her hands down her body, cupping her breasts, teasing her nipples into aroused points, loving the way he watched her, his expression rapt and intense. She pushed off from the jamb and sauntered toward him with a sinful glide of her hips, her eyes hot on his, her lips parted in anticipation. When she stood at the edge of the bed, she flipped the sheet back with a flick of her wrist. Then she reached out and trailed a single fingertip over his straining erection. A bead of clear fluid pearled beneath her fingertip, and she slowly spread it over the swollen head of his penis.

"My, my," she murmured. "Looks like something has indeed come up. Good thing I planned ahead."

"Damn good thing," he agreed huskily.

She'd meant to take her time, teasing him, arousing him, but clearly he was already well aroused, and God help her, so was she—from the moment she'd stood in the doorway and looked at him, lying in her bed, staring at her ceiling, his jaw darkened with morning stubble. It had hit her that tomorrow morning she'd be waking up alone, and she hadn't liked the realization at all.

She could take her time with him later. She wanted him inside her, and wanted him there *now.*

Reaching out, she snagged a condom from the ready supply on the nightstand, then climbed onto the bed, straddling him. After quickly rolling the condom over him, she guided his arousal to her wet opening and slowly sank down on him. Her eyes drifted closed, and her entire body seemed to sigh a single word: *Jackson.*

Resting her palms on her thighs, she rocked her hips, luxuriating in the shock of pleasure that rippled through her. His hips strained upward, pressing his erection deeper, shooting spears of heat to her core. She moved sinuously against him, watching him through half-closed eyes, savoring his absorbed attention.

He thrust deeply, eliciting a gasp of pleasure from her. Before she had the chance to draw a breath, he reared upright and fisted one hand in her hair, pulling her forward for a deep, lush mating of mouths and tongues. He filled his palms with her aching breasts, mercilessly teasing her aroused nipples. Leaving her lips, he kissed his way across her jaw, then trailed a fiery path down her neck, lower, to her breasts. A deep shudder racked her as he drew her nipple deep into the heated satin of his mouth, his tongue slowly swirling, each tug of his lips answered with a pull deep inside her. She wrapped her legs around his hips and let herself drown in the sensations bombarding her.

And then it seemed as if his hands were everywhere. Cupping her breasts. Gliding down her back. Gripping her hips. Exploring the contours of her buttocks. Slipping between their straining bodies to caress her swollen, sensitive flesh. Quivering with need, she tightened her legs around his hips, drawing them closer. He cradled her face in his hands, then drew her mouth to his.

"God, you feel so good," he breathed against her lips. "So hot. So wet. So tight."

"So hard. So deep. So…ooh." Her words turned into a moan as he thrust upward. She matched his ever quickening rhythm, the coil tightening inside her, until it broke, forcing a harsh cry from her lips. Grasping his shoulders, she arched her back, her orgasm throbbing through her, narrowing her entire world down to the exquisite place where his body joined intimately with hers. In some far corner of her mind, she heard him groan, grasp her hips tightly, felt him thrust deep, felt the shudders that shook him as he experienced his own release.

When her tremors subsided, she collapsed like a folded house of cards and leaned forward to rest her damp forehead against his. When she could draw a steady breath again, she leaned back and looked at him.

He brushed a curl from her cheek, tucking the tangled strands behind her ear, then trailed his fingers down her cheek. "Your skin is gorgeous. So soft."

She managed a smile. "All that milk I drink with my doughnuts and brownies."

"In that case, you're a walking testimonial to that

Milk Does A Body Good slogan. You should get a cut from the dairy industries." His fingers continued exploring, trailing over her shoulders then down her back to cup her buttocks. He gently squeezed her and winked. "Nice assets."

"Thanks." She pursed her lips and looked him over. "You know, seeing as how I'm an accountant, sex with me could possibly be considered a charitable contribution."

"Now *that* has got to be the greatest loophole ever." He dropped light a kiss onto her lips. "C'mon, Sweet Stuff. Let's hit the kitchen and check out that bacon. Thanks to you, I've worked up a ferocious appetite. After we've eaten, I may even let you have your wicked way with me again."

"Let me?" she scoffed. "Ha! Kiss my assets, Tennis-Man."

"Any time you want me to, sweetheart. Any time at all."

Riley looked into his eyes. Her heart performed a slow somersault and she irrevocably tumbled over the cliff. God help her, she loved him. Completely. His laugh. His smile. His sense of humor. His kindness and generosity. His intelligence and patience. His dedication to his job and his family. The way he made her feel.

But did he feel the same about her? He obviously liked her. Was it possible his feelings were as strong as hers? What would he do, what would he say, if she told him right here, right now that she loved him? The mere thought cramped her insides with trepidation. What if he said something bland like, *Thank you?* Or worse, *Yikes!* Or even worse, *See ya!*

Nothing bad could come of waiting, but all sorts of bad things could happen if she showed her cards too soon. Better to wait. He was leaving tonight, but they'd see each other again. She planned to visit him in New York next month, the perfect opportunity to get to know him on his own turf, and he'd come back to Atlanta. With the merger almost a done deal, Jackson's job would move to Atlanta, a prospect that filled her with hope for their future. Once she'd visited him, once the merger was settled, she'd tell him how she felt.

It was a good plan. So good, she refused to jinx it by considering that she'd need a Plan B.

11

WHEN JACKSON ARRIVED at work Monday morning—thirty minutes late, thanks to a subway delay—the office was already abuzz with the official news that had just come down via company e-mail: Prestige was merging with Elite Commercial Builders. The company would retain the name Prestige and consolidate its offices in Atlanta. The departments currently housed in the New York offices would be relocated. All New York employees would be offered either a relocation or severance package. A meeting was scheduled for tomorrow afternoon to discuss the particulars. Marcus wanted the transition and physical move to go as smoothly and quickly as possible, stating that three months was the goal.

Jackson poured a quick cup of coffee, then managed to escape the glut of employees in the break room, all of whom were huddled into groups discussing relocation options, and whether they planned to remain in New York or move. He entered his office, closed the door and pondered that very question himself. Of course, his decision depended on factors that were still unknowns—what sort of offer Prestige would make him, and if Winthrop Hotels would get in the game, too. And if Winthrop did make an offer, what it would be. When he'd come on board at Prestige, he'd known he'd most likely have to make this sort of decision. What he hadn't counted on was any other factors entering into his decision. Factors like Riley.

Damn it, he wouldn't, couldn't let the fact that she lived in Atlanta influence his decision. He'd worked too long and too hard to make a major career decision based on a woman he'd only known for a matter of weeks. If and when the time came, he would base his decision solely on what was best for his career.

His office phone rang, a welcome interruption to his unsettling thoughts. After picking up the receiver, he said, "Jackson Lange here."

"I just read the merger news," came Riley's voice. "Congratulations on your hard work paying off."

"Thanks." He leaned back in his leather chair and closed his eyes, picturing her in her office, dressed in some sort of pretty pastel summer dress, her long legs crossed, shiny hair brushing her shoulders, coffee mug sitting on her desk. An ache he couldn't put a name to squeezed him, the same ache he'd experienced lying in his bed alone last night. And waking up in bed alone this morning. "It's a good deal, and will propel Prestige into the big league."

"I agree. Of course, the next few months are going to be crazy while the transition is made," she said. "When I think of the accounting nightmare that is about to descend upon my department—integrating multiple systems, policies and procedures—I'm tempted to whup your butt for making this happen."

"Whup my butt? Promise?"

She laughed. "With all the work this will generate, I may never see the light of day again."

"I'll send you a box of light bulbs."

"I'd prefer doughnuts."

A vivid recollection slammed into him—of Riley, naked, gloriously flushed, tousled and rumpled after a steamy bout of lovemaking, offering him a bite of her of doughnut, then slowly licking the chocolate icing from his lips. He had to clear his throat to locate his voice. "I'll make a note of that."

"Since they want to move things quickly, I'm guessing you'll hear about your relocation offer soon. Probably this week."

"Probably," Jackson agreed. He didn't add that he expected to hear from Winthrop Hotels this week as well.

"I'd be happy to help you find a place here."

"I...I'd like that." *If it comes to that.*

An uncomfortable feeling invaded his chest, and it didn't take a genius to figure out what it was— guilt. Even though he hadn't lied, he still felt dishonest and it didn't sit well at all. But he didn't want to tell her until there was something to tell for fear that she'd say something like, *Please don't take another job in New York. Please move to Atlanta.* And he'd say, *Okay.* He couldn't risk making the wrong decision for the wrong reasons. And, as he was all too well aware, Riley was hell on his decision-making abilities.

His other phone line buzzed and shame filled him that he felt saved by the bell. "I have another call coming in," he said. "I'll let you know once I hear something." He should have ended right there, but before he could stop the words, they shot out of his mouth. "I miss you."

"Me, too," she said, her voice taking on a slightly sexy rasp that crowded a wealth of sensual images into his mind. "Bye."

"Bye." Jackson disconnected then drew a deep breath before picking up his other call. "Jackson Lange here."

"Jackson, this is Ted Whitman from Winthrop Hotels. I was wondering if you were free for lunch today."

Jackson consulted his schedule. "I am." After they agreed on the time and place, Jackson slowly replaced the receiver. Ted wouldn't ask him to lunch to tell him he wasn't being offered the position with Winthrop. Things were moving quickly. His hand was still resting on the phone when it rang again, this time with the beep that indicated an interoffice call.

When he answered, Paul Stanfield's secretary said, "Paul would like to see you in his office at three o'clock this afternoon if your schedule permits."

"Three o'clock is fine."

A meeting with the CFO. Most likely to offer Jackson a relocation package. Which meant that he'd have to make a very big decision—and even sooner than he'd thought.

ON TUESDAY NIGHT, Riley kept herself busy by folding laundry, cleaning the science experiments out of her refrigerator, vacuuming the dust bunnies under the sofa—anything so she didn't go nuts waiting for the phone to ring. She hadn't spoken to Jackson since her call to him yesterday morning, but she'd received a brief e-mail from him this morning saying he had news and he'd call her tonight after he got home from work.

Anticipation curled through her. Company scuttlebutt was rife with word that offers to the New York staff were being made and she was certain Jackson was going to tell her that he'd received his relocation offer from Prestige. Dozens of runaway thoughts and hopes collided in her mind, and she clicked off the vacuum to blow out a dreamy sigh.

Jackson moving to Atlanta. The magical time they'd already spent together continuing without the hindrance of distance between them. The two of them hunting for an apartment for him, or maybe— did she dare think it?—an apartment together. *Whew.* The mere thought sent jitters careening through her. But good jitters. Happy jitters that had a sheepish grin tugging at her lips. After waiting five years to finally have her apartment back to herself, even Madame Sees-All couldn't have predicted that she'd be filled with anticipation at the prospect of another roommate.

She dearly wished she really were a Madame Sees-All who could predict the future. Yet even though she didn't know *exactly* what the future held, she didn't doubt for a minute that her future included Jackson. She loved him. Wanted to be with him. Her reentrance into bachelorette-hood had been stunningly short-lived, but she was only too glad to abandon that plan. With Jackson, she felt more carefree and daring and happy than she'd ever felt before. She was ready to climb out on that limb and reach for the next branch.

She only prayed he'd feel the same way and she wouldn't fall out of the tree and break something— like her heart.

The phone rang, startling her from her dreamy reverie. She grabbed up the receiver and pressed it to her ear. "Hello?"

"It's me," came Jackson's deep voice. "Sorry it's so late. As I'm sure you can imagine, things at the office are crazy."

"They're insane here, too." Riley plopped down on her sofa and tucked her legs underneath her. "You sound really tired."

"I am."

An image of him, hair messed from plunging his fingers through it, tie loosened, top button of his white dress shirt undone, five o'clock shadow darkening his jaw popped into her mind, and she ached to touch him. "Wish I could give you a nice, long shoulder massage."

He huffed out a short laugh. "Not half as much as I wish you could."

Several seconds of silence stretched between them, then, unable to stand the suspense another second, Riley asked, "I guess you know I'm dying to hear your news. Did Prestige make you an offer here in Atlanta?"

"Yes."

"A good offer?"

"A very good offer."

Thank you, God. Riley briefly closed her eyes and absorbed the mental impression of her and Jackson together. Of her telling him she loved him, and him echoing the sentiment. Of her asking him to move in with her instead of finding a place of his own. Of their future together, filled with endless possibilities, laid out before them like a banquet feast.

She opened her eyes and smiled. "That's wonderful, Jackson. I can't wait until we—"

"There's more, Riley."

Something in his tone had her tightening her grip on the phone. "More?"

"I also received a job offer from Winthrop Hotels."

A frown yanked down Riley's brows at the name

of the well-known chain of luxury hotels. "Winthrop Hotels? How did that come about?"

"I interviewed with them the same day I traveled to Atlanta."

It took Riley a few seconds to digest that. "You never mentioned you were looking for another job, or that you'd interviewed for one."

"I figured it wasn't really worth mentioning unless and until there was something to mention."

"You didn't think the fact that you were considering leaving Prestige was worth mentioning?"

"I didn't want you worrying about something that might not even happen."

I…see," she said, although she was pretty sure she didn't. "Where is the Winthrop position located?"

"Here in New York."

"And I take it that since you're mentioning it now, you're considering their offer."

"It's a chief marketing officer position, Riley. One they created with me in mind. It's a big step up the ladder. You know how important that is to me."

"Yes, you made that very clear. But you said Prestige made you a very good offer."

"They did. Winthrop's offer was better."

The little dream bubbles floating above her head like bluebirds of happiness started to pop. Her throat tightened and she swallowed, hard, to relieve the lump of apprehension clogging her airway. Forcing a bright note into her voice that sounded strained to her own ears, she said, "Well, it sounds like you have some serious thinking to do. If you want to talk about it, I'd be happy to listen."

"I've already thought about it. I accepted Winthrop's offer this afternoon. I've spoken to Paul and handed in my resignation. He took it very well since based on our conversations he'd suspected I'd move on if the merger went through. We agreed I'll stay on for the next three weeks to help with the transition, and then I'll be—"

"Gone," she said, her voice flat. "You'll be gone." She squeezed her eyes shut and tried to pull in a deep breath, but her chest felt crushed. All the hope and happiness she'd relished only moments ago had been snuffed out like a candle tossed in a lake, replaced by an aching, suffocating hurt and, damn it, anger. Silence stretched between them.

"You're very quiet," he finally said.

"I don't know what to say."

"How about congratulations?"

"All right. Congratulations," she said without a lick of enthusiasm.

"I realize this is sort of unexpected—"

"Sort of?"

"Okay, maybe more than sort of, but it's water under the bridge, so let's just go on from here. I was thinking, how about if I fly down this weekend and we can—"

"No."

Jackson stilled at that single word uttered in that flat voice, a tone he'd never heard from Riley before. A trickle of apprehension crawled down his spine.

"What do you mean 'no'?" he asked slowly.

"I mean I don't want you to fly down this weekend."

His grip on the receiver tightened. "All right, then the following weekend."

"No. And not the weekend after that, or the one after that."

There was no mistaking the finality in her words, and he dragged his hand through his hair in frustration. "Riley, just because I didn't accept the position with Prestige doesn't mean we can't continue on as we have."

"Yes, I'm afraid it does."

"Can you please explain why?"

She drew in what sounded like a ragged breath, then said, "Because I don't want to continue on as we were. Because I wanted...more. Hoped for more. From you. For us." Her harsh, humorless laugh abraded his eardrum. "Oh, don't worry, your conscience is clear. You didn't lead me on or give me any reason to expect we'd ever be anything more than a notch on each other's bedposts."

A sharp pang of something he couldn't name, along with a healthy dose of annoyance, gripped him. "Damn it, Riley, you're not just a notch—"

"Yes, I am. The fact that you made this decision without even discussing it with me proves it. And proves exactly where I fit into your life and your priorities. And that's fine. I certainly can't begrudge you following your dreams and advancing your career. The problem is, I forgot to check my heart at the door." She let out a huff of breath. "But the fact that I allowed my feelings to become so...involved, well, that's my fault and my problem. I'll deal with it. But I don't want any further involvement in this...whatever sort of nonrelationship we've established. I'm done."

Jackson stood frozen in place, trying to assimilate everything she'd just said. Obviously she cared far more about him than she'd ever told him. And now she wanted him out of her life. "Riley, I didn't realize your feelings for me were that..." He pinched the bridge of his nose and shook his head. "Strong," he finished inanely.

"I can't see that it makes any difference. Unless…
are you saying you would have made a different decision if you'd known I was falling in love with
you?"

He closed his eyes, his heart rapping against his
ribs, afraid to examine the answer to that question because it hit so close to home. Hadn't he been afraid that
his intense feelings for her—feelings he didn't understand and feared would eventually burn out—might
influence his career-making decisions?

After exhaling a long breath, he said, "I couldn't
let feelings, either yours or mine, enter into such an
important decision regarding my career."

"Well. That pretty much says it all, doesn't it?"

"No, I don't think it does. Listen, it's late, we're
both tired. Let's talk about this tomorrow after we've
both had some sleep."

"There's nothing to talk about. Before you made
this decision, there would have been things to talk
about. But now, there's nothing left to say."

"Riley, even if we'd talked about it, I still would
have accepted the Winthrop job." He couldn't keep
the edge of frustration from his voice.

"Yes, you've made that perfectly clear. Which is
fine. But at least we would have discussed it. Shared
it. At least I would have known about it."

"So let me get this straight. It's not that you're
angry that I'm not moving to Atlanta. You're mad
that I did something without talking to you about it
first, even though I would have done the same thing
anyway."

Something that sounded like a cross between a
sob and a harsh laugh came through the phone line.
"Let me say this as clearly as I can, Jackson, so there's
no chance of you misunderstanding. I'm *hurt* that

you passed up an opportunity to come to Atlanta because I'd foolishly hoped we had something special together that had a chance of developing into more. I'm hurt and *angry* that you made the decision without even talking to me about it, without even mentioning that there might be another offer on the table. And I'm royally pissed at myself for allowing my feelings to get involved in a relationship that was clearly nothing more than sex on your part. The bottom line is you did what was best for you and that's that. And now I need to do what's best for me. You made your decision and I've made mine." The breath she blew out sounded decidedly shaky. "We're done."

Those two words hit him like a sucker punch. "Riley—"

"*Done.*" Her voice broke, and his heart turned over. "I don't want to hear from you anymore. Please don't call or e-mail me. It's over."

He felt like he'd been turned inside out. "I can't...damn it, you're crying."

"I'm not," she said in a trembling voice that belied her words. "But even if I were, it's not your problem. Good luck with your new job. I sincerely hope it makes you happy. Goodbye, Jackson."

"Riley, wait! This isn't...I don't want..." A sensation that felt unpleasantly like panic suffused him. "I can't just say goodbye like this."

"You don't need to. I already did."

Before he could say another word, the dial tone buzzed in his ear. He slowly lowered the phone, then dropped the receiver onto the sofa and dragged his hands down his face.

Jesus, he felt...gutted. Empty, yet somehow filled with an aching sense of loss that made his insides hurt in a way he'd never before experienced. He'd expected she might be upset. Disappointed. But he hadn't anticipated that she'd end their relationship.

Anger coiled its way through the hurt, and he grasped it like a lifeline. She didn't want to see him anymore? Hear from him anymore? Fine. Great. He'd made the right choice.

Hadn't he?

Another flash of irritation hit him for second-guessing himself. Yes, of course he'd made the right decision. He felt bad that he'd hurt her… A groan escaped him as the shaky sound of her voice echoed through his mind. Damn it, he hadn't ever meant to hurt her. Hadn't realized he would. That he could. But she'd made it pretty clear that she'd been…

Falling in love with him.

Another wave of loss rolled through him, and he sat down heavily on the sofa. Had she really? Well, if so, *had* seemed to be the operative word. Surely if she'd really loved him, she wouldn't have, couldn't have ended things so abruptly. So finally. And the fact that he had no intention of challenging her decision just proved that whatever his feelings for her were, they weren't love. Sure, he'd miss her—hey, they were great in bed together—but he'd move on. Actually, this was a good thing. In fact, he was relieved. Yeah—relief. That's what he was experiencing right now. The feelings, the emotions she inspired in him were too…powerful. Too confusing. Too overwhelming. Too distracting. Too…everything. *It's better this way*, his inner voice stated emphatically. *Really*.

Riley wasn't the right woman for him. Their relationship would have fizzled out soon anyway. Now he could go back to the life he'd had before she'd turned him upside down and inside out. This was good. Sure, right now it didn't feel so good, but that would pass.

Yup, it sure would.

12

"HOW ARE YOUR wedding plans coming along?"
Riley asked Gloria above the din in their favorite
Mexican cantina. It was an unseasonably warm Friday evening for late October in Atlanta, and they'd
stopped by after work for drinks and dinner. Her
gaze dropped to the gorgeous pear-shaped diamond
that had adorned Gloria's left hand for the past
month. Rob the tennis pro had turned out not only
to be a great guy, but to have excellent taste in engagement rings. And fiancées, Riley thought, shooting her friend an affectionate smile.

"Very smoothly, Miss Maid of Honor, so don't
worry," Gloria said, her eyes sparkling almost as
much as her ring. "Can you believe that in less than
six months I'm going to be a *bride*? A *wife*?"

Riley couldn't help but laugh at her friend's
dumbfounded expression. "Given that you're getting married, that can't come as a total surprise,"
she teased.

"I know, I know," Gloria said, waving around a
tortilla chip. "It just all still seems so...unreal. One
minute, I'm deliriously happy, then the next, I'm totally panicked. What if I'm not a good wife?"

"You'll be a fabulous wife. And Rob will be a wonderful husband."

Gloria's smile was absolutely loopy with love.

"Yeah, he will. And I knew it. Right from the first time I laid eyes on him, the first time I talked to him, I knew inside that he was *the one*."

A pang resonated through Riley which she firmly shook off. Had it only been eight weeks ago that she'd thought she'd found 'the one' in Jackson? Thank goodness things had worked out better for Gloria than they had for her.

"I can't wait to introduce you to Rob's friends," Gloria said, after devouring a salsa-laden chip. "Now that the initial merger craziness at work has settled down a bit, you don't have any more excuses to avoid meeting these men—these young, handsome, single, athletic men."

Riley forced a smile. "Sounds great."

Gloria reached out and squeezed her hand. "No, it doesn't," she said, her eyes filled with concern and sympathy. "And I really wish it did. But it will soon—it *has* to. It's been two months, Riley."

Riley didn't even pretend not to understand. She blew out a long sigh. "Two months, eight days, and nineteen hours," she said, picking up her salt-rimmed margarita glass. "And don't think I'm not royally pissed at myself for still moping." Damn it, the ache in her heart still hurt as much as it had the last time she'd spoken to Jackson two months, eight days and nineteen hours ago, a fact which really grated since Jackson had clearly moved on with his life.

"Well, one reason you're still hurting is that you've done nothing but work," Gloria said. "You need to get out and meet new men. Date. Where's that swinging, daring bachelorette who was supposed to emerge once Tara left?"

Oh, she'd emerged all right—and had taken a direct hit to the heart. "She's been buried under the avalanche of work brought on by the merger." And God knows she'd been grateful for the diversion. But it was time to move on. And she intended to do so.

"The best way to forget a man is to find another one," Gloria advised.

"That's the plan," Riley agreed. And she desperately wanted to forget Jackson. Unfortunately, she'd thus far been unable to do so. How could she forget when he was so firmly embedded in her mind and in her heart? Why didn't someone invent something useful like a love crowbar so that she could just pry Jackson out of her? "Now that work is under control, I'm anxious to jump back into the dating pool."

Hmm. Anxious was probably an overstatement. But after spending—okay, wallowing—the past two months in the brokenhearted pool, and eating way too many doughnuts, she was ready, or at least determined, to start meeting new men.

"One of Rob's friends is throwing a party a week from tomorrow. Why don't you come with us?"

Riley stomped down the immediate *no thanks* that rose to her lips and smiled. "Sounds like fun."

And she was way overdue for some fun. Jackson had moved on. It was time for her to do the same.

STANDING IN the corner of the gaily wedding-festooned reception hall, Jackson leaned one shoulder against the wall and watched the dancers circling the dance floor while the band played a slow, romantic ballad. Mom and Dad danced by, laughing like teenagers. And there were Mark and Jen, the bride and groom, smiling into each other's eyes. Jackson had never seen his brother so happy and as best man, he'd made mention of that fact during his toast.

"Sitting this one out?" asked Brian, joining him.

Jackson tore his gaze from the dancers and looked at his brother who, like him, was dressed in a black tux. "Takin' a breather," Jackson agreed, "although I don't know if there're any single women left that either Shelley or Mom haven't already tossed in my path." He nodded toward the extra beer Brian held. "That for me?"

"Yeah. You look like you could use it."

"Gee, thanks. And here I thought I looked all spiffy in my tux."

"The tux looks great. The guy wearing it looks like he needs a beer. You know, Shelley and Mom wouldn't be putting on the full-court press if you'd taken my advice and brought a date."

Brought a date... Yeah, he supposed he should have, but he hadn't been able to work up enough enthusiasm to ask anyone. In the past two months, he'd gone on three dates that he'd literally had to force himself to go on—which he'd mentally dubbed *The Trio of Dead-Boring Disasters.*

"Is everything okay with you?" Brian asked, his normally carefree expression fixed on Jackson with unmistakable concern. "You seem...unhappy. And you have for a while. Is the new job not going well?"

"Job's fine," Jackson said, wishing the statement was the whole truth instead of just half-true. Yes, his job with Winthrop Hotels was fine—challenging, interesting, great pay, great perks. He should have been on top of the world. Instead he felt...hollow. Unfulfilled. And achingly lonely. And in spite of filling every possible waking moment with work, his discontent, instead of lessening, grew stronger with each passing day.

God, he missed her. Every day. Every night. No matter how he tried to fill the hours, no matter how busy work kept him, Riley remained constantly in his thoughts. Had he actually believed two months ago that her giving him his walking papers was for the best? A humorless grunt rose in his throat and he took a long pull on his beer to drown it. What an ass he'd been. How many times had he picked up the phone to call her? Typed an e-mail only to delete it? A dozen? Two dozen? A hundred? But each time his pride had kept him from dialing, from hitting Send. She'd told him to get lost, and so he had. But damn it, that's all he'd felt ever since—lost. He'd tried to deny it, tried to tell himself the new job was wearing him out, he was just stressed. But he was tired of lying to himself.

He took another swig of his beer and returned his attention to the dance floor. Shelley and Dave danced by and waved and Jackson smiled in return. "Shelley looks great," he remarked to Brian. "Motherhood obviously agrees with her. You'd never know she's only averaging about four hours of sleep a night." His five-week-old niece Amanda was the most beautiful baby on the face of the Earth, but man, oh man, could that kid *yell*. But man, oh man, didn't she still look like an angel when she did.

"If the job's fine," Brian said, ignoring the change in subject, "then it must be girl trouble." When Jackson didn't respond, Brian continued, "Well, I'm feelin' your pain, dude. This chick I brought to the wedding, Cheryl? She's nice, we've gone out a few times, but I've only known her a month and she's suddenly hinting that she wants some sort of exclusive dating arrangement. This in spite of the fact that I told her upfront that's not my style." He shook his head. "Jeez. Is there anything harder to figure out than girls?"

"Yeah. Women."

Brian laughed. "I'll keep that in mind." He took a swig of beer, then asked, "Wanna tell me about whoever this woman is who has you so ripped up?"

Jackson shot him a sideways glance. "Who put you up to that question—Mom or Shelley?"

"Actually, neither one, but I'm sure they're dying to know." Brian scratched his head and frowned. "Gotta tell ya, bro, I don't get this whole falling in love thing *at all*. I mean look at Mark." He pointed his beer bottle toward their brother on the dance floor with Jen. "He's in love and as happy as a pig wallowing in a mud puddle. The guy does nothing but smile. You, on the other hand, are like the anti-Mark. You look like you've lost your best friend *and* your dog. You're obviously in love, but I've never seen you so miserable. I tell you, it's enough to make a guy run in the opposite direction. Especially if he's gonna end up like you."

Jackson went perfectly still. "What makes you think I'm in love?"

"Jeez, Jackson. You might as well have it tattooed on your forehead."

Well, hell. If Brian, who was not the most percep-tive of guys, had picked up on Jackson's feelings—feelings he'd steadfastly refused to put a name to—the situation had reached epic proportions. His brother had, with a simple statement, forced Jackson to face what he'd spent the last two months deny-ing—his feelings for Riley weren't just a simple case of sparks or lust. He was completely, totally in love with her. Had been since she'd knocked him flat the instant he'd laid eyes on her.

"So what's the story, Jackson? Why aren't you with this woman?"

Jackson didn't reply for several seconds, not quite sure what the answer to the question actually was. Finally he opted for an easy way out. "She lives in Atlanta."

"So?"

"Atlanta, *Georgia*."

"I didn't think you meant Atlanta, New York, dude. So she lives in Atlanta. Big deal. You know where the airport is. You have a phone. E-mail. Does she know how you feel?"

Jackson blew out a frustrated breath. "*I'm* not sure how I feel."

"For cryin' out loud, *I* know how you feel. How can you not? Listen, remember when Mark and Jen broke up for a month last year? How we were all ready to whack him because he was such a miserable, mopey pain in the ass? Well, now you're that same mopey pain in the ass. And do you remember what snapped Mark out of it?" Before Jackson could reply, Brian answered his own question. "He got back together with Jen. He was miserable because he loved her and he wasn't with her. They reunited and *whammo*—happy camper." Brian finished off his beer with a satisfied *aah*. "Think about it, man. I don't know the details, but seems like you've got nothing to lose. And oh, look, here comes Mom, with that matchmaking gleam in her eye. She probably just found out the caterer's aunt's neighbor has a single daughter or something. So glad I brought a date to save me. You're on your own, man."

With a jaunty salute, Brian sauntered off, and Jackson finished off his beer, his mind whirling.

He had a lot of thinking to do.

Because one way or another, it was time to take some drastic action.

THREE WEEKS after her dinner with Gloria, Riley sat in her office pouring over the budgets for next year, her take-out lunch container at her elbow waiting for her attention. A knock on her doorjamb had her lifting her head. Marcus stood in the open doorway, smiling.

"Lunch at your desk today, Riley?"

She smiled in return. "Yes, but not just any lunch. It's the turkey club from The Corner Bread Shop."

"I'll give you fifty dollars for it," Marcus said with a perfectly straight face.

"Forget it."

Marcus grinned. "I'm on my way out, but wanted to stop by with some news. We've *finally* filled the marketing head position. Took much longer than we'd anticipated, but we wanted the best man for the job. Jackson Lange was a tough act to follow."

Riley firmly ignored the arrow of pain that pierced her. "Someone from within?" she asked.

"No, we went outside the company. He's starting today. In fact, I just left him in his new office on the sixth floor. I told him I'd send you up so you can chat. Get the two departments off on the right foot. Good luck," he said then was gone.

Riley shot her sandwich a longing gaze, then resolutely rose to her feet and made her way toward the elevators. Best to get the introductions out of the way first. She didn't want to start off with another accounting/marketing battle like the one that had ensued with Jackson.

Jackson, Jackson, Jackson. When would she finally

stop thinking about him? Annoyed at herself, she stepped into the elevator and jabbed the button for the sixth floor, then squeezed her eyes shut. Bad idea. An image of Jackson, smiling, dark hair spilling onto his forehead, popped into her mind. She immediately opened her eyes and straightened her back.

Enough. She was done. The minute she returned to her office, she was going to dig through her purse for that business card, the one that handsome, personable man at Rob's party had given her along with a request to call him. What was his name again? Andy—that was it. She was going to call Andy. Go on a date with Andy. Yes, that was the plan.

The elevator doors slid open and she followed the Wedgwood-blue carpet to the marketing department's corner office. The door was open and Riley stood at the threshold. Boxes were stacked around the desk, file cabinets yawned open, and a new computer sat on the cherrywood desk. "Hello? Anybody home…."

Her voice trailed off and she stared, dumfounded as an achingly familiar figure rose from beneath the desk. "I'm home," Jackson said. He walked slowly around the desk, then leaned his hips against it, crossing his ankles. He raked his hand through his hair and offered her a tentative smile. "Just plugging in the computer wires."

Riley could only stare. He'd removed his charcoal-gray suit jacket, loosened his navy blue tie and rolled back the sleeves of his white dress shirt to reveal his strong forearms. He looked tall and strong and masculine and beautiful, and damn it, how was she supposed to forget him when he was *here*? That yanked her brows down and jerked her from her stupor.

"What are you doing here?" she asked, proud that her voice sounded almost normal.

"Trying to organize my office." He waved his hand, encompassing the dozens of boxes. "As you can see, I have my work cut out for me."

"Your office? I thought this office belonged to the head of marketing."

"It does." He offered her a jaunty salute. "Jackson Lange, head of marketing, at your service."

She looked around the spacious office and deafening silence yawned between them. A jumble of questions wrestled through Riley's mind and she fought to remain calm—at least on the outside. When their eyes met again, the impact hit her like a punch to the heart. He was studying her with a serious, unreadable expression that curled her toes inside her black leather pumps.

When she could trust her voice, she finally asked, "What about your job with Winthrop Hotels?"

"C'mon in and I'll tell you."

She hesitated for a second, then stepped over the threshold, skirting her way around several boxes until she stood near the window. He pushed off from the desk, then crossed to close the door. Riley's breath seemed to stall at the quiet click that ensconced them in privacy.

"I'd offer you a seat," he said with a lopsided smile, as he approached her, "but I don't have one yet."

"No problem. I'd prefer to stand anyway."

He didn't halt until no more than an arm's length separated them, and it was all Riley could do to hold her ground and not back up. She lifted her chin, and asked again, "So what's this all about?"

"I called Paul and Marcus two weeks ago to discuss employment opportunities with Prestige. When they told me they hadn't yet filled my old position, I asked for it. They agreed, I resigned from Winthrop, and here I am."

Riley frowned. "You weren't happy at Winthrop?"

"The job was great." His gaze searched hers, then he added softly, "But everything else was awful."

Her heart seemed to skip a beat, and she had to clamp her lips together to keep from blurting out, *Welcome to my world.* "Everything else?" she repeated. "What does that mean?"

"It means that I haven't felt as good in the last three months as I have in the last three minutes since you walked through that door. It means that since the day you told me you didn't want to see me or hear from me again, I've been miserable." He reached out and clasped her hands. The achingly familiar sensation of his palms against hers shot shafts of warmth up her arms.

"I'd finally made the career move I'd always wanted," he continued, his thumbs brushing slowly over the backs of her hands, "only to find out that it wasn't what I really wanted at all."

The serious way he was looking at her, the sensation of his touch, his words…and not a chair in sight. After moistening her suddenly dry lips, she asked, "What do you want?"

"You."

That single word seemed to reverberate in the room, and Riley had to lock her knees to keep from plopping down onto one of the boxes.

He raised her hands to his mouth and pressed a warm kiss against her fingers. "Nothing was right without you, Riley. *Nothing.* I tried my damnedest to fool myself into thinking that it could be, but I finally realized it was hopeless. I thought what we'd shared would burn out, but it's just continued to burn bright and steady. I love you. I want us to be together. More than any job, any career move. More than anything else."

Riley could probably count on one hand the number of times she'd been left utterly, totally speechless, but this just upped the number. Her heart felt as if it were flopping around in her chest, and she had to wonder if she'd really heard what she thought she had. Just to make certain, she asked slowly, "You've moved to Atlanta?"

His quick laugh blew warm against her fingers. "It would be a hell of a commute if I hadn't."

"So, after not contacting me for three months, you gave up your job, your apartment in New York and moved to Atlanta."

"To coin your favorite accounting phrase, that's the bottom line, yes."

"What makes you think I'd be happy about this decision—another one, I must point out, about which you didn't consult me."

"I don't know that you'll be happy about it. I only know that you told me you were falling in love with me and I hope you haven't changed your mind. I only know that I'm deeply, painfully, in love with you, and if your feelings have changed, I'm going to do everything I can to get you to change them back."

"You took a huge risk."

"I know. But I think the payoff is worth it." His dark blue gaze searched hers. "Have your feelings changed, Riley?" he asked quietly.

She considered the question for several heartbeats, then answered very seriously, "I'm afraid they have, Jackson."

There was no misinterpreting the pain that slashed across his features. A muscle ticked in his jaw and he looked down at the carpet. "I...see."

"I'm afraid they've grown stronger."

His head jerked up and their gazes collided. "Stronger?"

"Stronger," she repeated. "And not for lack of trying to make my feelings for you go away, believe me." She took a single step forward, halting when they almost, but not quite, touched. "Something happened to me the first time I saw you, Jackson."

"Probably the fallout from the blast that knocked me off my feet the first time I saw you."

Hot tears pushed behind her eyes. "I thought these feelings wouldn't last, but they've only grown more powerful. I love you," she whispered.

With a groan, he yanked her against him and lowered his mouth to hers. Her insides melted, and she clung to him, her senses all sighing with relief and love. When he finally lifted his head, they looked at each for several seconds. Then they smiled.

"Bloop," they said in unison, then laughed.

With his arms wrapped tightly around her, she waggled her brows and asked, "So what made you realize you couldn't live without me?"

"Believe it or not, it was a talk with my brother Brian that finally woke me up."

"He gives good advice?"

"God, no. He normally gives horrible advice. I've found that if I just do the exact opposite of whatever he suggests, everything turns out great. Instead of finding out what I should do, I find out what I shouldn't do, which leads me right to what I should do. But not this time. This time he was right on the money."

Riley smiled. "Sounds like the conversation I had with Tara the day she moved out. Seems that our baby siblings are growing up."

"Yeah. Maybe we should introduce them."

"I don't know if that's a good idea. It might be like two forces colliding."

"They'll meet each other at the wedding."

"Wedding? What wedding?"

"Our wedding."

Everything in Riley went perfectly still. She had to swallow twice to find her voice. "*Our* wedding?" she finally managed. "Um, what makes you think *I'll* be there?"

"Why wouldn't you be?"

She cocked a single brow. "Maybe the fact that no one has proposed to me."

Jackson closed his eyes and shook his head. "Damn. See what happens? I take one look at you and I forget what the hell I'm doing." To Riley's shock, he dropped to one knee before her. Clasping both her hands between his, he looked up at her with eyes so filled with love they stole her breath.

"Riley, I'm not sure how many people can say that they walked into a fortune-teller's tent and their life turned upside down, but I'm one of them. I love you. You make me laugh. You make me smile. Being with you feels so good, and as I've spent the last three months learning, being without you feels so damn bad. I love that we like different things and already you've taught me some great stuff about baseball and the finer points of eating a ball-park frank. I want to spend the next fifty years learning all about all the other stuff you like."

Riley's lips trembled and fat tears threatened to dribble from her eyes. Good God, this wonderful, romantic, beautiful man was killing her. With a shaky smile she asked, "What happens after fifty years? You plan to trade me in for two twenty-five-year-olds?"

He grinned up at her. "You and the math. It would have to be *three* twenty-five-year-olds since we'll both be about eighty by then. Think you'll still want me around, or will I get dumped for a boy toy?"

"Hmm. Depends on whether the boy toy can cook."

"Hmm. I guess I'll just have to keep reminding you you're not marrying me for my housekeeping skills."

She laughed. "That's the truth. Well, if it doesn't work out after the first fifty years, I guess we can conduct an audit at that time, reevaluate, and recommend an alternate course of action."

"Spoken like a true accountant. So what do you think?"

"I think you are the most incredible man I've ever met and I can't wait to be your wife."

He stood and pulled her into his arms. "Thank God," he whispered against her lips. "My knee was starting to hurt." Then his lips claimed hers for a deep, lush kiss filled with love and passion. When he lifted his head, he asked, "What does Madame Sees-All predict for us?"

Riley leaned back in the circle of his arms and smiled. "Love. Laughter. Joy. Children. Baseball. Tennis. And lots of doughnuts."

He laughed and hugged her against him. "Bring it on, Sweet Stuff. Bring it on."

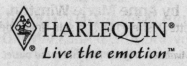

introduces an exciting new family saga with

DYNASTIES: THE DANFORTHS

**A family of prominence...
tested by scandal, sustained by passion!**